Isla,

Enjoy 😊

The Supervillain Next Door

Gary Smith

Gary.

ISBN-13: 9781794350519

For all the storytellers at St Columba's RC primary school, Cupar.

ACKNOWLEDGMENTS

Thank you to Julie Campbell for bringing Steve and his friends (and foes!) to such wonderfully expressive life. I'm grateful to the beta readers who gave me feedback, and have to acknowledge Luke and Ben's willingness to be bedtime story guinea pigs!

1

HERE COMES THE SUN

It had finally happened.

No one could quite believe their eyes.

After days and weeks where it had seemed that the rain would never end, the residents of Bridge Street opened their curtains and were greeted by a long-lost friend.

Bright sunshine.

The whole street sprang into action as one, as if someone had fired a starting pistol. In every house people wolfed down breakfast and pulled on their clothes, not even bothering to tidy up behind them.

Beds were left unmade, faces went unwashed and even the tidiest eaters left toast crumbs in the butter.

The drivers were out first, whistling happy tunes as they washed and polished their vehicles until they shone. Next were the gardeners, who rolled up their sleeves and got to work digging, planting and weeding.

But it was the children who were happiest to be venturing outdoors once again. Every game had been played with and book read cover to cover. Even computer games had started to lose their appeal.

So when the children realised that the sun was back they burst from their homes like a cheering and whooping tidal wave. Within minutes the street was full to bursting with kids of all ages. Some rode bikes or performed stunts on their scooters. Others simply lay on their backs and gazed up at the sky, huge goofy smiles plastered on their faces.

If asked, each child would have confidently declared that they – and they alone – were happiest to finally see the sun again.

All of these children would have been wrong.

Completely and *utterly* wrong. Because the boy who lived at number 9 Bridge Street, Steve Grant, was happiest of all.

For weeks, anyone passing number 9 and looking over the little stone wall would have seen a small face pressed against the window, desperately searching for any sign of blue sky.

What was the reason for Steve's window vigil, you might ask?

On the very day that the first drops of rain had appeared, he had finally completed the new glider that was his pride and joy. Sleek, shiny and lovingly painted, Steve knew that once in the air it would be the greatest flyer ever, leaving even the Millennium Falcon in its wake.

If it would only stop raining so he could try it!

Every night, Steve rushed through his homework as quickly as possible so that he could resume his position at the window. And hours later he would reluctantly tear himself away and trudge up the stairs for his bath, gloomily thinking that he couldn't escape water anywhere.

Every day brought more rain, with the puddles on the street increasing in size until they resembled tiny ponds. By the end of the second week, Steve was beginning to wish that he'd built a boat instead.

Perhaps the only benefit to those long hours of anticipation was that when the sun finally returned, Steve knew just how to mark the occasion: with the much-delayed maiden voyage of the Grant Glider 3000 (The actual name on the box was the SF-71, but Steve felt that his name was *much* better).

Ten years old, with a cheeky grin and a mop of brown hair that refused to be tamed, Steve was the kind of boy sometimes referred to by grown-ups as 'a real character'. He was always on the go, seemingly unable to sit still and concentrate for more than a few minutes at a time.

At school he always tried his best to listen to his teacher, Mrs Baxter. But no matter how hard he tried, his gaze would eventually wander to the classroom window. The world beyond, full of noise, smells and people bustling to and fro, made the silent classroom feel like a prison cell in comparison – one from which there was no prospect of escape.

What made school slightly more bearable was his best friend, Peter Rennie. The two had been inseparable from the day they'd met, getting into all kinds of mischief together. When Steve had opened the curtains to discover sunshine, he'd phoned Peter straight away.

The two of them stood in Steve's garden, Peter looking on admiringly as Steve showed off his creation. It was about half a metre long, painted black and red, with '3000' embossed on the tail section in large golden letters. The little plastic pilot stared out from within the cockpit, ready for action.

"The box says that it's meant to do stunts! We should try and make it loop the loop!"

"Do we have to?" asked Peter, twisting his hands together nervously. "You know how sudden movements make me feel queasy."

Steve shuddered, remembering the time that he'd persuaded Peter to go on the waltzers. That was a mistake he'd *never* make again. Normal rain was bad enough but a vomit shower was even worse.

"Oh, come on, it'll be fun! Just watch – I bet I can do all kinds of tricks."

Steve picked up the glider and strode to the centre of the garden, with Peter following nervously behind. He drew back his arm with the glider poised for take-off, the sunlight reflecting off its red stripes.

"Mission Control, we are cleared for launch. 5, 4, 3, 2, 1, **GO!**"

Steve launched the glider into the air and it shot upwards, darting and turning through the sky. The boys watched, transfixed, as it looped around and flew towards them, with Steve jumping to catch it.

"That was awesome!" he exclaimed, hopping from foot to foot with excitement. "I told you it would work!"

"Yeah, that was great," enthused Peter, his earlier worries now forgotten. "Can I have a shot?" he asked, sticking his hand out.

Steve hesitated. Peter was a good friend – his best friend - but he was also the most accident-prone person he'd ever met.

"I don't know, Pete. I mean, you are pretty clumsy.

Remember how you lost my frisbee? And when you gave me back my Transformers, one was missing a head and one had no feet."

"Oh, that was ages ago," Peter protested, his face the picture of innocence. "You can trust me, I promise I'll be extra careful."

Steve reluctantly handed over the glider, hoping that he hadn't just made a terrible mistake.

"And here's Space Captain Peter Rennie setting off on another thrilling adventure. **KAPOW!**"

Peter launched the glider into the sky and it twisted and turned, momentarily hanging suspended in the air before dropping straight towards next door's fence.

"Pete, grab it!"

The two boys ran forward, desperately trying to intercept the glider's descent. As it fell Steve took one final despairing leap, his outstretched fingers just brushing the tail of the glider as it flew past. He landed on the ground with a thud that knocked the breath from him, and could only watch helplessly as his prized possession sailed over the fence and into the neighbouring garden.

Steve clambered to his feet and dusted himself down, a horrible sinking feeling in the pit of his stomach. Peter pulled up behind him, puffing and out of breath.

"Oops, sorry about that! Shall we go and ask for it back?"

Steve stared at him in utter disbelief, his eyes almost popping out of his head.

"Ask for it back? ASK FOR IT BACK? Do you have any idea whose house that is?"

Seeing the crazed expression on Steve's face, Peter took a step backwards. "Erm, your neighbour's?" he squeaked.

Steve grabbed Peter's arm and pulled him towards the fence, ignoring his vigorous protests.

"Oh, he's not just any old neighbour, the man's a monster. Just look!"

Peter was far from convinced that he wanted to see whatever terrible sight awaited him, but he did feel rather guilty about losing Steve's glider. He grudgingly heaved himself up to look over the fence, his arms shaking with the strain.

The sight that greeted him wasn't *quite* as bad as he'd been expecting. An elderly man lay stretched out on a garden chair, engrossed in reading a newspaper. His balding head glistened with beads of sweat, a sun hat sitting unused on his lap.

He was wearing a pair of black shorts that were so faded they were almost see-through, matched with a frayed string vest that might have been white once upon a time.

Steve's glider lay at the side of the chair. Focused on his paper, it seemed that the man had yet to notice it.

Peter dropped down to the ground, increasingly puzzled. "It's just an old man. Ask for the glider back and he'll throw it over. He'll hardly even have to move."

"I wish it were that easy," sighed Steve. "Watch this."

He put a foot on the fence and pushed himself up until he could see over. "Mr Hunter," he called. "Could you throw back my glider, please?"

The old man carefully folded his newspaper and placed it to one side, before sitting up and swinging his legs onto the ground. He used his hat to fan himself as he stood up and Peter could make out dark bushy eyebrows attached to his face like two sleeping caterpillars.

"Your glider, eh?"

Mr Hunter looked around him and let out a cry of satisfaction when he spotted the glider. He picked it up and examined it closely, a smile newly appeared on his face.

"This is pretty nice," he remarked admiringly, turning it over. "Is it new?"

"Today's the first time we've flown it," replied Steve. "Can you throw it back to us?" He nudged Peter and the two of them flashed Mr Hunter their most angelic smiles.

"Oh, that's just too bad," sighed Mr Hunter. "I would like to but I know I've told you before what happens to toys that I find in my garden."

He looked at the boys expectantly, waiting for an answer, but Steve was unusually silent, staring down at the ground. Peter tried to fill the gap. "You give them back to their owners?"

"BWAH HA HA"

Mr Hunter erupted with laughter and Peter chuckled uneasily, not quite sure what was so funny.

"I'll make it nice and simple for you to understand, tubby. Finders keepers!"

Placing the battered hat back on his head, he picked up his newspaper and the glider and began to walk towards his house, tunelessly whistling to himself.

The boys watched him go and Peter turned towards Steve in disbelief, hardly able to believe what he'd just seen.

Steve kicked the fence in frustration, the delight and excitement of earlier now a distant memory. "That man," he fumed, "is the reason I don't like old people."

2

THE BOY AND THE BIG MEANIE

Bet that made you spit out your Ribena, didn't it?

You probably read that and thought: 'Doesn't like old people? He can't say that!' In fact, right now you're probably writing an outraged letter to the Prime Minister or to Justin Fletcher, telling them how old people are brilliant and that your granny makes the most fantastically tasty bowl of custard.

And you're right – most old people are awesome. The world is full of amazing grannies and grandads, not to mention those nice old people that always carry sweeties in their pockets. And the Queen is so amazing that they put her on all the money AND let her own all the swans.

But it's a sad fact of life that there are always a few rotten apples and, unfortunately for Steve, Mr Hunter could best be described as a big meanie.

Not just your normal everyday meanie - the kind who might steal your place in the lunch queue or 'accidentally' kick a football in your face. Oh no, Mr Hunter was a meanie of legendary proportions.

He was the MOUNT EVEREST of meanies.

He was the GRAND CANYON of meanies.

How mean was he? So mean that the brainiest of scientists would have to invent a whole new category of meanness simply to describe what a rotter he was.

In short, Mr Hunter was not a nice man.

Two years ago, when Steve and his Mum had first moved to Bridge Street, their new neighbours had welcomed them with open arms. The doorbell had constantly rung with people introducing themselves or offering help, and Steve had quickly befriended the other kids on the street.

It soon felt like they had been living there for years,

with the other neighbours becoming familiar sights.

- Mr Muggins from number 22, who was always on his bike and waved at Steve whenever he saw him, wobbling from side-to-side as he did so.

- Miss Johnstone from number 14, who always wore sunglasses whatever the weather and Steve suspected might be a vampire.

- The Meiklim family from number 33, who all squashed inside a battered old Ford Fiesta. Their black Labrador always stuck its head out of the window, its ears flapping in the wind.

But while the residents of the street quickly became an extended family for Steve, one mystery still remained. He had yet to meet his next-door neighbour at number 8.

Sometimes he would catch a glimpse of someone moving about inside, see a door close or hands pulling curtains together. But he never saw the house's occupant and couldn't wait to meet his mysterious neighbour.

He'd soon learn to be careful what he wished for.

One baking hot summer afternoon, Steve was sat

reading a book in the shady spot underneath their old oak tree. He let out a sigh of satisfaction as the persistent drone of Mr Parry's lawnmower faded away. Finally, some peace to concentrate on his book!

He had only read a couple of pages when another noise caught his attention, this time from over the garden fence. Curious, he put down his book and looked over, just in time to see the backdoor of number 8 open and someone step into the garden.

Steve's pulse quickened. Was this his elusive neighbour? Intrigued, he tiptoed towards the fence for a better look.

What he saw was an old man wearing a thin grey cardigan and faded blue cords. His feet were stuffed within the backless slippers that old people love, meaning that he had to shuffle slowly forward to avoid them coming loose. In his right hand he carried a plastic bag which swung back and forward as he walked, its contents knocking together.

The old man muttered to himself as he opened the lid of his plastic bin, forcefully squashing down the cartons and bottles inside. He threw his bag on top of the rubbish and pushed it downwards, before dropping the bin lid with a BANG that made Steve almost jump out of his skin.

"What was that? Who's there?"

The old man peered over the fence into Steve's garden. He raised his walking stick and held it like a weapon, waving it back and forth.

It was the first time that Steve had been threatened with a walking stick and he wasn't quite sure what to do. Laugh? Faint? Run away? Eventually he just felt rather silly and stood up, giving the old man an embarrassed wave.

"Hi there," he smiled. "My name's Steve, I'm your new neighbour."

Normally when Steve introduced himself to a grownup the reaction went one of two ways. They would smile politely and then try and find an adult to engage them in 'proper' conversation, or they would talk to him like he was a toddler, oblivious to how daft they sounded.

The reaction this time was a little more unusual. The old man jumped back in horror, his face turning a funny shade of purple. He jabbed an accusing finger in Steve's direction, spitting out his words in hysterical horror.

"You're a boy! You! My neighbour! A boy!"

Steve wasn't quite sure how to respond to this. The man looked really upset and he had no idea why. Steve was the first to admit that he could get a bit grubby at times, but today he was practically spotless.

"That's right. I'm sorry, would you rather I was a girl?" Steve gave the old man a big grin, hoping that humour would put him at ease.

It didn't.

"A boy! Germs! Noise! Slugs, snails and puppy dog tails!"

The man furiously marched towards Steve, hardly appearing to notice when his slippers flew off and lodged themselves inside a nearby bush. He stopped beside the fence, so close that Steve could almost count the long black hairs that sprouted from his huge nostrils.

"Excuse me!" protested Steve. "I am not made out of slugs and snails. Anyway, I was just trying to be nice by saying 'Hello'. Almost wish I hadn't bothered now."

"NICE?" roared the man. "NICE?" He lifted his walking stick and rapped it on the fence, beating it in time with his words.

"You are a little boy, you are not nice." **RAP**

"You are noisy and messy and will no doubt disturb my peace!" **RAP**

"And who knows what you'll do to my garden. Probably fill it with crisp packets and lolly sticks. And destroy all my flowers with your football!" **RAP**

"Bogeys! You'll pick your nose and leave bogeys all over my beautiful fence! Big green bogeys that you'll excavate from your nostrils and stick on my fence until it turns green!" **RAP**

"I-" **RAP** - "do-" **RAP** - "not-" **RAP** - "want-" **RAP** - "a-" **RAP** - "green-" **RAP** - "fence!" **RAP**

By now, Steve was convinced that his new neighbour was a fully paid up resident of crazy town. Being shouted at by a grownup was quite nerve-wracking and he automatically wanted to apologise, but then something stopped him.

This man was talking crazy, accusing him of all

sorts of things. Why should he apologise for things that he hadn't even done? He didn't even pick his nose!

Well, at least not in front of anyone else.

Steve raised himself up to his full height of 4 foot 7 and puffed out his chest. "You're not being very nice," he argued. "I'm going to be a really good neighbour, but only if you try to be one too. I am nice, I don't drop litter and I'm not going to leave bogeys on your fence."

They stared at each other across the fence for some time, neither saying a word, until Steve felt compelled to break the awkward silence.

"I don't think you've told me your name? I'm Steve Grant."

The old man examined him coolly and then took a step back, adjusting his cardigan in an attempt to regain his dignity. "If you must talk to me then you can call me Mr Hunter," he sniffed. "But I'll warn you now that I don't want anything to do with you."

He walked over to the bush and, with some difficulty, leaned over to retrieve his slippers from among the branches. He slipped them on and turned towards Steve once more.

"Just so you know, if I find either you or any of your belongings on my property there will be consequences. Do we understand each other?"

Steve swallowed nervously. He wasn't quite sure what that meant but he was sure it wasn't anything good.

"Yes, I understand."

"Excellent!"

Mr Hunter gave a chilly smile and turned his back on Steve without another word, heading back up the garden. Steve watched him all the way, not daring to take his eyes off him until Mr Hunter had opened the door and vanished inside his house.

When Steve was sure that the old man wasn't coming back out he sank down to the ground, letting out a huge sigh of relief. His neighbours had all been so nice that he should have expected there would be at least one bad apple on the street, but why did it have to be in the house next door to him?

3

ON ENEMY TERRITORY

Steve sat at the kitchen table, gazing mournfully into his glass of Ribena. His Mum was chattering on about the good weather and the latest gossip she'd heard from neighbours, but all that Steve could think about was his glider.

Why did he have to have Mr Hunter for a neighbour? It just wasn't fair! Old people were meant to be nice and kind, and maybe smell slightly of cabbage. They weren't meant to be crazy weirdos who stole all of your toys.

The glider, his football, his NERF bullets, his frisbee.

Between Mr Hunter keeping his toys and Peter breaking them, he'd be lucky if he had any left soon. The thought made Steve even more depressed and he let out an almighty groan, resting his forehead on the cool surface of the table.

His Mum stopped what she was doing and turned towards him, suddenly concerned. "Steve, is something the matter?"

"Yes, Mum. Our neighbour is a nasty old toy-stealing meanie pants. He has a face like a hippo's bottom and nose hairs so long you could use them as a rope swing."

At least that's what Steve wanted to say. But his Mum was so happy to finally have a day off that the last thing he wanted to do was upset her. The other problem was that his Mum and Mr Hunter were... well, not friends exactly, but at least on speaking terms.

Steve's Mum worked as a driver for the local Age Concern, spending most of her day transporting old people around town. As she never got tired of telling Steve, some of these people lived by themselves and their time with friends at the Age Concern might be the highlight of their week.

And one of her regular passengers was – you guessed it – Mr Hunter. He was often at the Age Concern, with his favourite game apparently being dominoes. Steve hoped that they frisked him on the way out to make sure he wasn't stealing any of the pieces.

This meant that whenever Steve tried to talk about Mr Hunter, his Mum would always butt in before he could get the words out. He would want to complain about his being mean and stealing toys but would soon find himself nodding sympathetically as his Mum said how lonely he must be living in that big house by himself.

Steve doubted that anyone would want to live with Mr Hunter and thought he would probably be the worst housemate ever, but felt it best to keep that view to himself.

His Mum sat down next to him, putting her arm around his shoulders and pulling him close. Steve was so depressed that he didn't even make his usual complaint that he was getting far too old for cuddles.

"Come on, Steve, what's the matter with you? It's not like you to look so down, especially when it's so nice outside."

She clicked her fingers as a thought occurred to her.

"I know, why don't you get that glider you built and we can throw it around outside. Let's see if your old Mum still has a good throwing arm."

Put on the spot, Steve was torn over how to respond. Turn down his Mum's offer and hurt her feelings, or tell her the truth about Mr Hunter and shatter her illusions that he was a lovely old man.

"One teeny problem with that, Mum. I've kind of... lost the glider."

***

Ten minutes later, Steve and his Mum were standing on Mr Hunter's doorstep, waiting for him to answer the door. Steve shifted awkwardly from foot to foot, wondering how on earth he had ended up here.

He'd told his Mum what had happened to his glider, leaving nothing out, and had expected her to be outraged at Mr Hunter's behaviour. Instead he'd been horrified to find that she'd stuck up for the old meanie! His Mum had confidently declared that it must be a big misunderstanding and that Mr Hunter probably picked it up by accident.

Which is why he was now on enemy territory outside Mr Hunter's home. Steve muttered to himself in frustration. Maybe it wasn't just old people. Maybe all grownups were crazy.

As the seconds ticked by with no response his Mum rang the doorbell again, keeping her finger pressed on the buzzer. After a few moments they heard movement inside and her grip on his shoulder tightened. Steve guessed it was either a warning to be on his best behaviour or an attempt to stop him running away.

There was the rattle of chains and the sound of locks being turned and unbolted before the door swung open to reveal Mr Hunter. Standing in the doorway, resting on his walking stick and wearing his tatty slippers, he looked just like a typical old man. Steve knew better.

"Why, if it isn't my favourite bus driver," he

simpered, turning on the charm. "What brings you to my humble abode?"

"We're very sorry to bother you, Mr Hunter, but Steve has something to ask you. I think there's been a little misunderstanding."

Steve stared at his Mum in disbelief, his mouth hanging open. What did she think she was doing? What did she expect him to say? She gave him a forceful nudge in the back and he grudgingly turned towards Mr Hunter.

"Can I have my glider back, please?" he muttered.

Mr Hunter's face broke into a Cheshire cat grin and he chuckled to himself. "Why of course you can, my dear boy. I was just about to bring it over! Wait here for a second."

He retreated back into the house and quickly reappeared brandishing the glider. He raised it into the air, making aeroplane noises as he passed it over to Steve.

"There you go my lad. When I found it in my garden I noticed that the tail had come slightly loose, so I took the liberty of fixing it for you. It was going to be a surprise but the main thing is that you've got it now."

Steve looked at Mr Hunter in astonishment, amazed that he could tell such a barefaced lie. His Mum, on the other hand, was delighted and made a big show of thanking Mr Hunter for his thoughtfulness.

As she thanked him again and they said their goodbyes, Mr Hunter waved enthusiastically as they walked back out of his garden.

Steve's Mum turned to him, smiling broadly. "What did I tell you? I knew there'd be a simple explanation. We're lucky to have such a thoughtful neighbour."

She put her arm around Steve and pulled him close. "I don't think he's got any family, so he probably thinks of you as the grandson he's never had."

Steve looked over his shoulder and saw Mr Hunter still standing in the doorway. When he noticed Steve he stopped waving and put his fingers to his eyes, miming wiping away tears. Then he put a hand on his belly and rocked back and forward with silent laughter.

Steve let out a strangled gargle and his Mum turned around to see Mr Hunter waving politely at them both.

"Oh yeah," muttered Steve. "He thinks I'm special all right. I think he's one of a kind as well."

"Marvellous!" smiled his Mum. "Aren't we lucky to have such nice neighbours?"

Steve bit his tongue and tried *very* hard to think nice thoughts.

4

SURVIVING SCHOOL DINNERS

At school the following day, Steve's mood hadn't improved much. Although he tried his best to concentrate all he kept thinking about was how Mr Hunter had managed to fool his Mum so easily. The man wasn't just an old meanie he was practically a criminal mastermind!

Mrs Baxter tried her best to bring him into the class discussion, but each time she asked him a question it was obvious to everyone that he hadn't been listening. After the third attempt she gave up and began directing her questions at Jenny Wishart and the other brainiacs who always had their hands in the air.

As Jenny droned on, giving her answer in excruciating detail, Steve's thoughts were interrupted by someone whispering his name. He turned around and inwardly groaned when he saw that it was Jill Mckenzie. As always, she looked insufferably smug.

She leant forward, one hand playing with her long brown pigtails.

"You're so stupid, Steven. Even a *five-year old* could have answered these questions."

Jill had been in his class since primary one and in all that time had yet to say a nice word to him. Steve found her *incredibly* annoying and sometimes wondered if she and Mr Hunter were related.

"How many times do I have to tell you – it's Steve, not Steven! Using long words doesn't make people think you're any smarter you know."

"And how would you know that? Your favourite book is still *The Hungry Caterpillar*!"

"It is not!" shouted Steve indignantly, hoping that Jill wouldn't ask if he still owned a copy. "And your favourite book is probably *The Guinness Book Of Records*, because you have the record for being the most annoying girl on the entire planet!"

"STEVEN GRANT!"

Steve looked round to see Mrs Baxter striding towards him with a face like thunder. Before he had a chance to mutter an excuse she had reached his desk and was looming over him, her displeasure plain to see.

"Steven, if my lesson doesn't hold your interest then perhaps your time would be better spent somewhere else."

That actually sounded quite good to Steve. He looked at her suspiciously, wondering what the catch was.

"In fact, why don't you go along to the headteacher's office and tell him exactly why I've sent you."

Steve could feel everyone in the class staring at him, with Jill trying to hide her obvious delight that she'd helped make this happen. With as much dignity as he could muster he collected his things together and walked out of the classroom, heading to meet Mr Spence.

***

The clock on the wall ticked away to itself as Steve and Mr Spence sat looking at each other. Steve had heard that this was one of Mr Spence's favourite tricks – 'thinking time' so that pupils could reflect on whatever offence had brought them to his office.

Not that Steve was thinking too hard about what he had done wrong. As far as he was concerned he was the innocent victim - if there was any justice in the world then Jill Mckenzie would be sitting here instead.

Mr Spence sat in his high-backed leather chair with his arms folded across his chest, his eyes fixed on Steve. Bored and impatient, Steve stared back, examining him closely. He'd always thought that Mr Spence seemed quite young for a headteacher. He had round thick-framed glasses and short dark hair, and compared to some of the other teachers his suit seemed clean and reasonably new.

"Do you want to tell me what happened, Steve?"

he enquired, unfolding his arms and tapping his fingers on the arms of his chair.

"There's not much to tell," muttered Steve. "I was just a little noisy in class, that's all."

"I see. And why is that? Are Mrs Baxter's lessons not enough to hold your interest?"

Steve swallowed nervously, not liking where the conversation was headed. "They are, Sir. It won't happen again."

"See that it doesn't, Steve. I know that school may not always be the most exciting place, but it will benefit you in the long run – particularly if you pay attention! In fact, I used to-"

Any further words of wisdom from Mr Spence were interrupted by the clanging of the lunch time bell. Seeing Steve's wistful gaze toward the closed door and realising the hopelessness of his cause, he gestured Steve to stand up. "Go on then, away and get your lunch."

Steve didn't have to be told twice. He was out the door almost before Mr Spence had finished speaking, grateful that at least one of his teachers was almost human.

***

When Steve entered the canteen he spotted Peter in the queue. He ran over and squeezed in beside him, pretending not to notice the sullen glares from those behind them in the line.

"How did you get on?" asked Peter as he collected his cutlery and condiments. "Are you in trouble?"

Steve smiled, hardly able to believe his luck. "No, it was fine; Mr Spence isn't so bad. I'm just glad he let me go for lunch – I'm starving!"

The two boys followed the line along until they reached the hot food counter. Dinner lady Mary was in her normal position, scooping portions of food onto children's plates and looking as if she'd rather be anywhere else. Her eyes were barely visible behind the dirty lenses of her large, thick glasses, while strands of unruly grey hair poked out from beneath her green hat.

Steve watched as Grace Pairman was served a heaped spoonful of mince, despite protesting that she was vegetarian and couldn't eat it. Mary gave her a hard stare, saying nothing, and Grace scurried away, gingerly holding her plate at arm's length.

When Steve reached the counter he held out his plate and gave Mary his most charming smile. "I'll have a Panini, please."

Mary scooped a spoonful of mince onto Steve's plate and then added another one for good measure. Steve bit his tongue as she added the potatoes and vegetables. He knew by now that it was useless to complain.

Back at their table, Steve and Peter sat looking at their meals. Steve was starving and could hear his stomach gurgling and groaning, but even his famously robust appetite had its limits.

He looked down at the unappetising portion before him. The mince lay in a puddle of grease and the lonely scoop of mashed potato was lumpy and cold. But the smell was the worst thing – like sweaty gym socks mixed with overcooked broccoli.

The last time that Steve had dared to try the school mince he'd felt ill for two days afterwards. There was no way he was going to make that mistake again. He pushed it away and consoled himself with the fact that his Mum was making sausages tonight. At least that was something to look forward to.

Steve watched as Mr Spence entered the room and began talking to Mary. Expecting to see him presented with the same horrible slop, Steve was amazed to see Mary hand over a delicious looking plate of burger and chips. That definitely hadn't been on the menu – obviously being the headteacher brought some perks.

"Can you believe this, Pete?" he complained, warily poking his mashed potato with his fork. "What I can't work out is how someone can work as a school cook for so many years and still be utterly terrible. Aren't you supposed to get better at cooking with practice?"

Peter didn't reply, totally focused on devouring his mince. Steve tried his hardest not to gag as he watched each new mouthful go down.

Peter eventually noticed Steve's look of disgust and paused, his fork suspended in the air. "Sorry, did you say something? I'm starving, I forgot to bring a snack today."

He looked over at Steve's full plate. "In fact, I don't suppose you wo-"

"Just take it," sighed Steve, pushing the plate towards Peter who gratefully received it.

The two boys sat in silence for a time, the only sound being Peter's contented chewing, before Steve smiled and turned towards his friend.

"Pete, call me crazy but I've got an idea."

Peter dropped his cutlery with a clatter, his face suddenly turned ghostly white.

"Please don't say that! I know all about your ideas – they normally finish with something going wrong and us getting into trouble."

"They do not!" protested Steve. "Well, not always."

He leant in closer to Peter and spoke in a low whisper.

"I think I know how to get all of my toys back from Mr Hunter, but it might be quite risky."

"When is one of your plans not risky?" moaned Peter. "Just remember when it all goes wrong that I warned you what would happen!"

5

A FANTASTIC DISCOVERY

"I'm not sure about this, Steve," complained Peter, remaining rooted to the doorstep. "Isn't this breaking and entering? And what if he comes back?"

Steve stopped in his tracks and let out a groan of frustration. He'd already explained the plan to Peter over and over again. Couldn't he just trust him for once?

"Pete, we've been through this. All we're going to do is take back what's mine. That's hardly stealing, is it? In fact, Mr Hunter only has my things because he stole them!"

"Well, I suppose so..."

"And we know that he's left to pick up his paper, like he does every day. And that it always takes him about twenty minutes to get there and back."

"I guess twenty minutes is quite a long time..."

Steve could tell that Peter's objections were weakening and played his trump card. "And it's not breaking and entering for one simple reason. We have a key."

Steve put the key in the lock and turned it, not waiting to hear Peter's reply. His Mum had spare house keys for several of the old people that she transported, and he was sure that she wouldn't mind him borrowing Mr Hunter's. After all, she *had* been wanting them to spend more time together.

"Well... okay. If you're sure." Peter followed Steve into the house, carefully closing the door behind him.

The two boys stood in the unfamiliar hallway and looked around them. At first glance, nothing seemed out of the ordinary. The house was clean, tidy and very boring, with nothing out of place. The walls were practically bare, with a small mirror in the hall appearing to be the only decoration.

Hoisting his schoolbag on his shoulder, Steve set off, tiptoeing from room to room like a ninja master of stealth. Peter placed his bag on the floor and followed after him, occasionally glancing nervously over his shoulder towards the closed front door.

After a short time they had looked in every room and searched in every nook and cranny, but there was still no sign of Steve's missing toys.

"I don't think they're out here," whispered Steve. "I think we should start looking in cupboards."

With a weary sigh of resignation, Peter headed to the kitchen and Steve soon heard the sound of doors being opened and closed. Looking around for somewhere else to check, his gaze fell upon the cupboard underneath the stairs.

Curious, he pulled open the door and fumbled for the light switch. The bulb gradually flickered into life, illuminating the cupboard's contents, and Steve froze, surprised at the sight that greeted him.

The cupboard was empty, with none of the coats and shoes that he'd been expecting to see. Instead there were stairs leading downwards into the darkness.

"Pete, you better come and see this," he called, still trying to peer into the gloom.

Peter emerged from the kitchen and burst out laughing when he saw where Steve was waiting. "A cupboard under the stairs! Don't tell me, you've found Harry Potter."

"Not exactly," replied Steve. "Have a look."

He moved to one side and gestured down the stairs into the inky blackness. Peter peered down and gave an impressed whistle. "Wow, that looks like it goes down really deep. I didn't think any of these houses had basements."

"Neither did I," mused Steve. "That's why I'm really curious to find what he's got down there."

There was another light switch at the top of the stairs, but Steve flicked it back and forth without visible effect. After a brief search he found a dusty torch in the corner of the cupboard and switched it on. It emitted the faintest of glows.

"Are you sure about this, Steve?" asked Peter,

anxiously checking his watch. "Mr Hunter will be back any minute now and who knows what he's got down there."

"That's why we've got to look," Steve argued. "He could have been stealing things off kids for years. He shouldn't be allowed to get away with it."

He walked forward onto the first step, the wood creaking beneath his feet. Carefully, Steve tiptoed down the staircase, using the pale light of the torch to illuminate his path. Peter followed close behind, resting one hand on Steve's shoulder to keep his balance.

When the two boys reached the bottom, Steve shone the torch around the room. It was larger than he'd expected and filled to bursting with objects, but it wasn't the skateboards and toys that he'd hoped to find.

As the torchlight danced over the room each shaft of light revealed a new discovery. The walls were covered in photographs and framed newspaper clippings, while display stands around the room were filled with strange gadgets, outlandish costumes and exotic looking jewellery.

"Look around this place," Steve squealed, practically bouncing up and down with excitement. "Don't you know what this means?"

Peter brushed a cobweb away from his face and coughed as it dislodged a thick cloud of dust. "That Mr Hunter really needs to hire a good cleaner?" he choked.

Steve shook his head. "Just look at all this stuff" he exclaimed, casting his torch light from one strange object to the next. "This isn't just a basement - it's a secret lair! Mr Hunter isn't just a grumpy old man. He's a grumpy old supervillain!"

6

INSIDE THE SECRET LAIR

Peter burst out laughing at Steve's impassioned declaration. "A supervillain? Steve, don't be crazy! Mr Hunter looks like he'd get blown away in a strong wind."

Peter actually thought the idea was about as likely as a dog learning to play the trumpet. Still, he felt bad when he saw the hurt look on Steve's face and tried his best to let him down gently.

"I know Mr Hunter's a bit of a grump, but think of it this way. Do you know any other supervillains? Do you even know any superheroes?"

"Well, no..." admitted Steve, beginning to feel rather foolish.

"Well if we haven't heard of superheroes and supervillains existing in the big cities, how likely is it that you end up with a supervillain living next door to you?"

"Okay," pouted Steve, sticking out his bottom lip. "You don't have to keep going on about it."

Peter laughed, enjoying the novelty of Steve listening to him for once. "Sorry, it's just kind of funny. He's probably a hoarder – you know how old people love to collect random things. My Nana Jones has the creepiest doll collection that you could ever see."

He turned to go back up the stairs, still chuckling to himself. "Come on. Supervillain or not, we better get out of here before he comes back."

Not waiting for Steve to follow, Peter took a step forward but stumbled in the gloom. He fell forward and threw his hands out to support himself, and as he did so his outstretched fingers brushed a switch on the wall. A humming sound appeared that built in intensity and then lights suspended in the ceiling flickered to life, slowly illuminating the basement and its contents.

The two boys looked around the room in amazement, hardly able to believe their eyes. Peter hurriedly picked himself up and ran towards Steve, grabbing his arm tightly.

"Okay, I believe you," he stammered. "Can we please go now?"

Steve barely heard him. He was too busy looking around the room, captivated by his surroundings. The torchlight had hinted at the room's contents but even that hadn't prepared him for the reality.

Unlike the bare walls upstairs, those in the basement were covered with countless photographs and newspaper clippings, some framed and others crudely stuck on, the browning sellotape slowly losing its hold on the wall.

But that wasn't what had caught Steve's attention. Dotted around the room were glass cases and display cabinets, and from the nature of the contents within Steve knew that his suspicions about Mr Hunter had been correct.

The tall glass cases contained brightly coloured costumes, as if ripped straight from the pages of a comic book. The smaller display cabinets were crammed with strange looking machinery and gadgets, everything from shiny metal orbs to what looked like futuristic jewellery.

"Don't touch anything," Steve whispered to Peter. "We have no idea what this stuff is."

Steve carefully blew the cobwebs away from a framed picture and examined it closely. It was an old newspaper cutting reporting on a bank robbery that had been foiled by a superhero. In the accompanying picture, The Defender smiled for the camera while holding on tightly to the captured villain, The Mischief Maker.

Is that who you are? wondered Steve, peering at the Mischief Maker's masked features. *But why would you want to keep souvenirs of the times that you lost?*

The Mischief Maker and The Defender appeared in other headlines, as did many other heroes and villains. Captain Danger, Madam Mesmera, Reason Lad, The Dancing Fool – So many names were featured again and again, with their fights and deadly plans shouting out from the headlines.

Steve read each one with mounting confusion. It seemed that his small town had once been home to enough heroes and villains to rival any Marvel comic, so why hadn't he heard of them? Even if they were all old now, like Mr Hunter, surely people would still talk about them and their exploits.

Lost in thought, he moved over to examine some of the costumes contained within the glass cabinets. He recognised some as belonging to the people in the newspaper clippings, both hero and villain, but in real life they were so much more colourful and eye-catching. They were just how he'd always imagined such costumes would be, with large boots, flowing capes and branded belts.

In a daze he wandered over to the display cases. One object that caught his eye looked like a ray gun, with ornate studded gems surrounding the long barrel. But it couldn't possibly be real, could it? The thought both scared and excited Steve.

Less unusual was a silver ring, looking totally out of

place among the strange gadgets and colourful costumes. Steve's curiosity got the better of him and he cautiously picked it up before examining it closely. There were no marks or inscriptions on it, nor fancy stones – it appeared to be just a normal ring.

His thoughts were interrupted by a call from the other side of the room.

"Erm, Steve... I might need some help here."

"Yeah, okay. I'll be over in a minute," Steve distractedly replied, his attention still focused on the ring.

"No, now please."

Steve stopped what he was doing and looked round. It had almost sounded like there was a touch of panic in Peter's voice and for a moment he worried that Mr Hunter had come back early.

He wasn't reassured by the fact that Peter was nowhere to be seen.

"Pete, are you there? Come on this isn't funny."

Starting to worry about his friend, Steve slipped the ring into his pocket and crept forward, his eyes scanning the room. He couldn't see Peter anywhere and began to fear the worst. Then he caught sight of something black and furry on the floor, sticking out from behind a display case in the corner of the room.

Gathering up his courage he stealthily edged closer, creeping forward inch by inch until he was face-to-face with the mysterious object.

A badger – the largest one he had ever seen. (Actually, it was technically the only one he had ever seen in real life, but Steve was too surprised to fuss over minor details.)

Steve didn't know a lot about badgers but he was reasonably confident of two facts. Firstly, they were often described as quite grumpy animals. Secondly, they weren't normally found in houses.

He stood frozen to the spot and scared to move, but it soon became apparent that the badger barely seemed to notice him. Its paws were raised as if it was examining them closely, and it was making soft snuffling noises. If it didn't sound so crazy then Steve would almost swear that it was crying.

"Pete," hissed Steve. "Come and see this!"

The badger raised its head and looked at Steve,

and there was something about its dark eyes that looked almost human. It held up its large paws and looked at them sadly.

"Steve, I think I touched something," it said, in a voice that sounded very familiar.

Steve looked at the badger.

The badger looked back at Steve.

"Pete?" said Steve to the badger, feeling rather silly.

"Hi Steve," sighed the badger. "I told you that things would go wrong."

7

A REMARKABLE TRANSFORMATION

I'm dreaming, thought Steve. *Any minute now, Mum will come and wake me up and then I'll have something nice for breakfast.*

He screwed his eyes shut and pinched his arm as hard as he could. Then he warily opened one eye.

The badger was still there, staring back at him. It lifted a paw up and waggled a claw in his direction as if telling him off. "Whenever you're ready, Steve, I would appreciate some help turning back to normal."

Taking a deep breath, Steve forced himself to move forward until he was as close to the badger as he dared. "What have you done now?" he asked in exasperation.

"I didn't mean to touch it," protested Peter. "It just looked so lovely and shiny and I wanted a closer look. How was I supposed to know this would happen?"

He folded his paws in front of his chest, looking very sorry for himself. Steve had never seen a badger sulk before but he was finding it a day of many surprises.

Steve looked at his watch and groaned - Mr

Hunter would be back any minute! The plan had turned into a *total* disaster. He was in a supervillain's lair, his best friend was now a badger, and he still hadn't found his toys. What on earth were they going to do?

Then Steve had a brilliant idea.

"Pete!" he shouted, excitedly waving his arms about. "Where's the thing that transformed you? Maybe it can turn you back."

Peter pointed towards the corner of the room, not even bothering to raise his furry head. "I think it rolled over there. Badgers don't have thumbs you know, which makes it hard to hold on to things... and play video games... and brush your teeth... and-"

"Alright I get the picture!" Steve got down on his hands and knees and shone the torch across the floor, illuminating every nook and cranny. At first the light revealed nothing apart from dead spiders and dust, until eventually it picked out something glittering underneath a display case.

Steve stretched forward to reach for the object but then thought better of it. His Mum probably wouldn't appreciate having a badger for a son. Changing tack, he delved into his school bag and pulled out a folder, using that to edge the object back towards him.

What emerged from the darkness was a sparkling broach with a dark green emerald inside, its vibrant colours entirely unaffected by the surrounding dust. The shades of colour that danced within were mesmerising, almost hypnotic, and Steve had to force himself to look away.

"Is this what you touched?" he asked Peter, gesturing to the broach.

Peter looked up and recoiled in horror. "That's it," he stammered, "keep it away from me!"

"Pete, just think about it," Steve urged. "If touching this turned you into a badger, maybe touching it again could turn you back to normal."

"Or it could turn me into something else," moaned Peter. "A badger is bad enough, but what if it turns me into a mouse or a skunk or something really horrible?"

Steve checked his watch again. They were cutting this far too close for comfort. "Just touch it, Pete.

Now!"

Peter stretched out a hairy limb and placed his paw on top of the emerald. A green glow appeared that grew in intensity until it enveloped him, forcing Steve to avert his eyes. When he looked back, blinking away the dark spots that had obscured his vision, he was incredibly relieved to see Peter standing before him once again.

Peter's school uniform was a crumpled mess and his normally tidy hair was sticking up like he had just cuddled an electric eel. He held up his hands in front of him, studying them warily as if making sure they were actually his.

"How do you feel?" Steve asked him.

"Okay, I think," Peter replied, patting himself all over to make sure that all his body parts were present and accounted for.

Very carefully, Steve placed the edge of the folder under the broach and levered it up, before placing it on top of a cabinet in the far corner of the room. It had done more than enough damage for one day.

"OH NO!"

Steve heard Peter's shout and whipped round, afraid to think what trouble his friend had got himself into this time. If he'd been turned into an animal again then Steve hoped it would be a dog this time. He'd always wanted one.

Peter was holding up his jumper and polo shirt, examining his belly with a look of great indignation. "This is terrible," he groaned. "My belly button has changed from an innie to an outie – my life is ruined!"

Steve chuckled with relief. "If that's the worst that's happened then I think we've had a lucky escape. Come on, let's get out of here."

The two friends began to make their way towards the steps and then froze in their tracks.

From upstairs came the unmistakable sound of the front door opening.

Heavy footsteps pounded on floorboards and keys rattled, before the door slammed shut.

There was silence for a time as both boys held their breath, hardly daring to move. Then the sound of footsteps resumed, moving deeper into the house.

A terrible thought entered Steve's head and he

grabbed Peter by the arm, his eyes wide and staring. "Pete," he hissed. "Where's your schoolbag?"

Peter gave him a reassuring smile. "Don't worry! I left it by the front door so that I wouldn't forget it when we left."

Steve slapped his forehead in disbelief and Peter blushed as realisation slowly dawned. "Maybe he won't notice it?" he said hopefully.

As if on cue a loud voice could be heard from upstairs. The unmistakable tones of Mr Hunter.

"Steven Grant, is that you? Just wait until your mother hears about this!"

They heard the creak of floorboards as Mr Hunter moved from room to room, opening doors and banging cupboards.

"And is your tubby little friend here as well?"

Peter cradled his belly, visibly upset. "He called me tubby," he complained. "That's not very nice."

"Of course he's not very nice!" hissed Steve. "He's a supervillain, remember? He's hardly going to give you pony rides and free lollipops!"

"What do we do?" shrieked Peter, flapping his arms

in distress. "We're trapped down here. If he catches us he'll probably turn me into a badger burger!"

Steve's thoughts whirled and whizzed round his head as he tried to think what to do. Stay put and try to hide, or make a break for it and hope for the best?

His mind made up he grabbed Peter's arm and pulled him towards the stairs. "Come on, we'll try and sneak out. He's old – I bet he won't even hear us."

Steve turned off the light and the two stealthily crept up the basement stairs. Each footstep sounded like an explosion and each creak like a scream, but the two boys gritted their teeth and continued their journey.

They eventually reached the top of the stairs and emerged into the small cupboard. Now only a thin door separated them from the hallway and the nearby presence of Mr Hunter.

They both stood stock still, hardly daring to breathe. No sounds came from the hallway, no footsteps or threats, and the boys looked at each other, trying to silently decide their next move.

Steve's throat was dry as he carefully pushed the

door open a crack and eased his head out, looking all around the hall. Mr Hunter was nowhere to be seen.

"Come on, let's go!" Steve whispered. He squeezed himself out of the cupboard and ran towards the front door, Peter following closely behind.

They reached the door without encountering Mr Hunter, hardly able to believe their luck. Peter carefully picked up his schoolbag and Steve put his hand on the door handle. He pushed down.

Nothing happened.

He tried again, pushing down with all his might until his arms ached. The door refused to cooperate, remaining stubbornly closed.

"Can't you get out? Oh dear, perhaps these would help."

The boys turned around to be confronted by a grinning Mr Hunter, the keys to the front door dangling from between his fingers.

"Two trespassers in my house. Whatever am I going to do with you?"

8

CAUGHT RED-HANDED

"Run!"

Steve pushed Peter in front of him, running deeper into the house in a mad dash to escape Mr Hunter.

"Where are we going?" panted Peter as they dodged past the chairs and tables in the living room, their hearts pounding in their chests until they felt ready to burst.

"Head for the back door!" shouted Steve. "It might be unlocked!"

Steve charged into the kitchen, hot on Peter's heels. Risking a quick look over his shoulder, he was relieved to see that Mr Hunter was nowhere in sight. For a moment he even dared to hope that they'd managed to outrun him.

The happy illusion didn't last long.

Mr Hunter stood in front of the back door, his hand resting on Peter's shoulder. Peter stood stock still with an expression of pure terror on his face, and Steve could see Mr Hunter's bony fingers digging into his shoulder.

"I hope you weren't planning on going somewhere, Steven?" smirked Mr Hunter. "You've only just got here."

"Let Peter go, Mr Hunter," Steve said, trying not to show how scared he felt. After what they had found in the basement he had no idea what the old man was capable of.

"And why would I do that?" Mr Hunter asked, his voice dripping with sarcasm. "You both came to my house after all – don't you want to see me?"

Steve seethed in silent frustration. He was normally full of clever plans but he had no idea what to do now. Even if he managed to find help from a grownup, Peter and he would still look like the bad guys for being in Mr Hunter's house.

The impasse was broken from a most unlikely source.

From the moment that Mr Hunter had caught him, Peter had been too scared to move. As Mr Hunter and Steve had talked the fears and worries had built up inside him until he couldn't take it anymore.

"You're not turning me into a badger!" he screamed, wriggling and struggling as he tried to extract himself from Mr Hunter's clutches.

His attention focused on Steve, Mr Hunter was caught momentarily off guard and almost lost his grip. But he regained his composure and grabbed Peter by both shoulders, spinning him round to face him.

"A badger? What are you talking about, you stupid boy?"

"You can't turn people into badgers – it's not right! I'm a boy. I'm a human boy!"

Mr Hunter turned to Steve, his annoyance plain to see. "I think your friend is broken. Do you have any idea what he's babbling on about?"

"Gee, I don't know," replied Steve. "Maybe the fact that you're a supervillain? We know all your secrets."

The old man looked at Steve in disbelief and for a moment there was silence in the room, followed shortly thereafter by the sound of laughter.

Mr Hunter rocked back and forward in amused delight, emitting a loud booming laugh. Steve had never seen Mr Hunter this happy before and found it a most unnerving sight.

"You think I'm a supervillain? Oh, you silly boys – why on earth would you think that?"

"We're not silly boys," Steve protested. "We found your lair with all your inventions. We know what you can do."

"Yeah, turn people into badgers!" Peter interrupted. "I'm sure my hands weren't this hairy before," he mused, examining them closely.

If this had been an episode of *Scooby Doo*, this would be the point where the villain admits their wrongdoing and confesses their evil plan.

Mr Hunter's reaction was somewhat different.

"You really are the most horrible little boys. I am NOT a supervillain and I DON'T have a secret lair. I simply don't like annoying, naughty children – WHICH BOTH OF YOU ARE!"

Steve wasn't particularly surprised that Mr Hunter denied the accusation - after all, villains were meant to lie. What annoyed him was a grownup treating him like he was a stupid child who could be tricked and bamboozled.

Trying to show a confidence that he didn't feel, Steve walked up to Mr Hunter. Standing on his tiptoes, he spoke slowly and deliberately. "You do have a secret lair and we've both been in it. It's down in your basement."

Mr Hunter laughed, appearing totally unconcerned. "Nice try, boys, but there's just one small problem with your theory: I don't have a basement."

"You do so," argued Peter. "We've both been down it. That's where I was turned into a badger."

"Why do you keep rabbiting on about badgers?" Mr Hunter snapped. He released his grip on Peter and gave him a shove forward. "Right, you – the tubby boy. Show me this magical basement that I'm supposed to have."

Peter glanced nervously at Steve as he passed, who did his best to return a reassuring smile. Mr Hunter pushed Steve in front of him and the mismatched trio walked into the hallway, coming to a stop in front of the door.

"Here you go," said Peter. "The door to the basement."

Mr Hunter looked where Peter was pointing and his lip curled in displeasure. "You're either playing a trick or you're as crazy as a fruit loop. What a waste of my time."

"What do you mean?" asked Steve. "The door's right there."

Mr Hunter looked at him with disgust. "My boy, I may be old but I am not blind. That is a solid wall, there is no door there."

Steve and Peter looked at each other in confusion. The door was in front of them as clear as day, what was Mr Hunter playing at?

"There is a door there," ventured Steve, pointing towards it. "See?"

"Boy, you have nearly exhausted my patience. There is no door there!"

"Yes there is, you know there is. Leading down to your secret lair."

"My secret la-? Oh, for goodness sake! Go on then, show me this magical door!" Mr Hunter gestured Steve forward and then folded his arms, looking even grumpier than normal.

Steve walked towards the cupboard door until he was standing before it. He grabbed the door handle and pulled it hard, the door swinging open with a loud creak.

A choking gurgle came from behind him and Steve looked round to see Mr Hunter staring at the door in disbelief. His mouth was hanging open and his eyes were bulging, his hands now hanging limply at his side.

"There you go – that's your cupboard under the stairs. Are you still going to try and tell us that it's not real?"

Mr Hunter didn't answer. In fact, he barely seemed to hear Steve's words at all. He walked toward the open cupboard as if in a trance, stepping inside and looking about him in amazement.

"What's going on?" Peter whispered to Steve. "What's he doing?"

Steve hadn't the faintest idea. Mr Hunter was now in a world of his own, having seemingly forgotten they were even there. It would have been the perfect opportunity for Peter and him to make their escape but he was intrigued, curious what Mr Hunter was going to do next.

Mr Hunter looked around the cramped interior of the cupboard, his fingers tracing the walls and finally coming to rest on the light switch at the top of the stairs. "This feels familiar," he muttered to himself. "So familiar."

The boys watched as Mr Hunter pressed the light switch and stepped forward on to the staircase.

The staircase that was still in darkness due to a faulty light switch.

"I rememb – WOAH!"

They heard the shout of surprise and then the crashing and banging that signalled Mr Hunter's unorthodox method of climbing down the stairs.

Steve and Peter ran into the cupboard and raced down the stairs, learning from Mr Hunter's mistakes and taking care to hold onto the handrail. When they reached the bottom they turned on the switch and the lights flickered on to reveal Mr Hunter lying in a crumpled heap.

"Oh my gosh we've killed him, we're going to jail!" squeaked Peter, turning a sickly shade of green as he looked down at Mr Hunter's still form.

"No we haven't, he'll be fine."

"Where's that broach? I can turn myself into a badger, the police won't be looking for a badger."

"Pete, just calm down."

"It won't be such a bad life. Living outdoors, getting plenty of exercise."

"Pete, just listen to me-"

"Frolicking with my woodland friends."

"Pete, just-"

"Climbing trees and eating nuts."

"PETE!"

"What is it?" grumbled Peter. "Can't you see I'm planning my new life here?"

"Well for starters, badgers don't live in trees or eat nuts – you're thinking of squirrels. And more importantly, he's okay – look!"

The two boys watched as Mr Hunter's prostrate form began to stir. He unsteadily rose to his feet, groaning softly as he massaged his head. But when he caught sight of the objects scattered around the room it was as if his injuries were instantly forgotten. A new spring in his step, he hurried forward and began examining them intently one by one.

"We're for it now," gulped Peter. "He's probably deciding what gadget will do the most horrible thing to us."

"Mr Hunter," called Steve, hesitantly. "Are you okay, Sir?"

Mr Hunter turned to face Steve and gave him a beaming smile. "I'm better than okay, my boy, I'm wonderful!"

"Okay... why is that?"

"Because I've remembered something very important."

The boys watched in astonishment as Mr Hunter stood with his legs apart and placed his hands on his hips, tilting his head upwards and thrusting out his chin.

"I, am a SUPERHERO!"

9

MEANIE NO MORE

Steve looked at Peter.

Peter looked at Steve.

They both looked at Mr Hunter.

He was still standing in his superhero pose, legs apart and chest puffed out, waiting for their reaction to his announcement.

Peter leaned closer to Steve. "What's he talking about?" he whispered. "Do you think he banged his head?"

The two boys watched as Mr Hunter began to wander around the room, occasionally emitting chuckles of delight as he examined the strange collection of objects and pictures.

"This is really weird," Steve mused. "He actually looks happy."

"He must have banged his head harder than we thought," muttered Peter.

A whoop of delight came from the corner of the room as Mr Hunter came across the mounted costumes. His eyes sparkled as he looked them up and down, his hand pressed lovingly against the glass case.

"Should we sneak off?" asked Peter. "I think he's forgotten that we're even here."

"We can't do that," Steve replied. "What if he's really hurt? We can't just leave him on his own."

"He'll be fine," argued Peter. "This is the man who's made your life a misery. He's perfectly capable of being left by himself."

Steve watched as Mr Hunter removed the strange looking gun from the display case and lifted it up, examining it closely. A beam of piercing blue light shot out from the barrel and struck one of the newspaper cuttings on the wall, blowing a smoking hole through the centre of the paper. Mr Hunter swiftly put the gun down and moved to a different part of the room, whistling innocently.

"Oh yeah, he's *totally* capable," Steve sarcastically replied. "Mr Hunter – can we talk to you for a second?"

Mr Hunter hurried over to them, smiling broadly. "Of course, boys," he replied. "What can I do for you?"

"You could answer a few questions for us if you don't mind," asked Steve.

"Absolutely!" Mr Hunter beamed. "Anything to help."

"You're a superhero," began Steve.

"That's right," smiled Mr Hunter. "The Defender, at your service."

Steve and Peter exchanged glances, remembering how The Defender had been in several of the photos and newspaper clippings scattered around the room.

Mr Hunter noticed their expressions and a flicker of concern crossed his face. "What's the matter?" he asked. "Is something wrong?"

Steve shifted from foot to foot, feeling rather awkward. "Well, the thing is, I'm not trying to be cheeky but it's a little hard to believe that you're a superhero. You've always been really mean to me."

Mr Hunter gasped and clutched his chest, looking horrified at the mere suggestion. "Mean to you? Why that can't be true, I love children!"

"Excuse us one second." Steve smiled politely at Mr Hunter and then grabbed Peter by the arm, marching him to the corner of the room.

"Okay, I am now officially weirded out. What's happened to him?"

Peter looked over at Mr Hunter, who gave a cheery little wave when he spotted him. "Concussion?" he ventured.

"We definitely can't leave him alone with all the gadgets here. Give him five minutes and he might blow up the whole street!" Steve gulped, hardly believing what he was about to say. "We'll have to take him back to my house."

Pretending not to notice Peter's frantic gestures and hissed protests, Steve walked over to join Mr

Hunter who beamed with delight when he saw him.

"Mr Hunter, I was wondering if you'd like to come over to my house for a cup of tea. I'd love to hear some of your superhero stories."

"You would? Well I would be honoured to visit your homestead. Lead the way, Simon."

"It's Steven, actually."

"Of course it is," chuckled Mr Hunter. "Just what I meant."

Steve and Peter exchanged worried glances as they followed Mr Hunter up the stairs.

***

Ten minutes later, Steve and Mr Hunter were in Steve's kitchen, Peter having made his excuses and left for school. Steve sipped his glass of Ribena while Mr Hunter's cup of tea lay untouched as he looked around the room, delighting in every picture and drawing that he found.

"You have a wonderful home here, Steven," he boomed. "Thank you for inviting me over."

"You're welcome," replied Steve, shifting uncomfortably in his seat. He glanced at his watch and wondered what the school would think when he explained that he had been late because he was babysitting a crazy and possibly superpowered old man.

"Can I ask you some questions?" Steve enquired. "I've got to be at school soon, so I don't have much time."

Mr Hunter pulled out a chair and sat down across from him. "Of course, my boy. It wouldn't do for you to get into trouble on my account."

Steve wracked his brain for a good question but found it hard to know where to start. "You're a superhero?" he eventually asked.

"That's right," replied Mr Hunter, smiling proudly.

"So why didn't you remember that before today?"

"I'm afraid I don't know."

"Okay, why do you think you couldn't see the entrance to your secret lair?"

"Sorry, I don't know that either."

"Right, well if you are a superhero why have you been such a horrible neighbour to me?"

"I don't know – that doesn't sound like me at all."

Steve rolled his eyes in frustration. As interviewees went, Mr Hunter was about as much use as a chocolate teapot.

"Okay, let's start with something nice and easy. If you're a superhero, what kind of powers do you have?"

Mr Hunter rolled up his sleeve and looked quizzically at his scrawny arm. "I had super strength, I think, but I guess I'm just an old man now. And it might sound odd, but I'm sure that I could fly."

Steve watched as Mr Hunter lifted up his cup of tea, his hand shaking slightly as he took a sip. It was hard to picture him ever having super strength – at the moment he looked just like any other old man.

Had Mr Hunter ever had powers? If so, had they faded over time? Was he stronger than he looked?

Steve knew one question that might shed some light on the matter. "How did you get your powers in the first place?" he asked.

Mr Hunter put down his cup of tea and gazed into the distance, his mind travelling back to days gone-by. "Now that's quite a story. Listen closely and I'll tell you all about it."

10

MY SUPERHERO ORIGIN

"It all started when I was a teacher at Blackwood Academy."

"Wait, that's my school!" exclaimed Steve in surprise. "What did you teach?"

"Gym."

Steve was silent for a moment, pondering this new nugget of information. If Mr Hunter had been a gym teacher then that *definitely* made him more likely to be a supervillain.

Mr Hunter didn't appear to notice, lost in his memories.

"It was a great school to teach at. I loved working with the pupils and the staff were all great. There was one in particular who was the most beautiful girl I'd ever seen-"

"Yes, yes, very good," interrupted Steve, pulling a face. "I'm sure your love life is fascinating, Mr Hunter, but I'd rather hear about the superpowers you say you had."

"Right, sorry," muttered Mr Hunter, growing visibly flustered. "I was in the gym hall with Billy. He kept forgetting his gym kit so I'd held him back to help tidy up. We were just putting the cones away when we found it."

"Found what?" breathed Steve, tingling with excitement. "Was it an alien? Was it a treasure map leading to an ancient artefact? Was it a magical potion?"

"Not exactly," admitted Mr Hunter. "It was a sock."

"A sock?" exclaimed Steve in horrified disbelief. "You got your superpowers from a magic sock?"

"A green sock to be exact," explained Mr Hunter. "We found it in the corner of the equipment store, underneath a bag of footballs."

Steve wasn't quite sure how to respond to this. Superheroes were meant to have memorable larger-than-life origin stories, not get their powers from smelly gym socks.

"You're absolutely sure it was the sock?" he probed. "There wasn't a wizard hiding in the shadows, or maybe a radiation leak in the boiler room?"

"Not that I know of," answered Mr Hunter. "Billy touched it first but was too disgusted to actually pick it up. When I did, the strangest thing happened. I threw the sock towards the bin and it smashed straight through it.

"I lifted up the bin to have a closer look and almost threw it up to the ceiling. Then I noticed Billy pointing at my arms. I'd always been quite fit, but all of a sudden my muscles were huge. I looked like something from a cartoon."

Despite himself, Steve found himself getting caught up in the strange story. "So, what do you think happened, exactly? That this sock made you super?"

Mr Hunter smiled ruefully. "I suppose that's one

way of putting it. You could say that it made me into the best version of myself, but not all the effects were as visible as my muscles. I'd always loved making things and I'd later find that I could dream up the most unusual inventions."

Turning someone into a badger certainly counted as unusual and Steve was tempted to ask why that had ever seemed like a good idea. Then a more important question popped into his head.

"Mr Hunter, what about Billy? You said that he touched the sock as well - did anything happen to him?"

Mr Hunter chuckled to himself. "Ah, now that's a good question! Billy always had a way with words – in fact, he was the star of the school debating team. But after he touched the sock it became even more noticeable. He could talk people into doing anything he said."

Steve thought about what he would do with such a power – how he would convince teachers that the dog really had eaten his homework and persuade his Mum that he didn't have to spend his Saturday morning cleaning his room.

Mr Hunter must have guessed what he was thinking because he gave him a stern look and wagged his finger. "Remember, young man, superheroes must only use their powers for good. That's why once Billy and I realised what we could do, we decided to become superheroes and help others. We called ourselves The Defender and Reason Lad."

As outlandish as the story seemed, some of the pieces were starting to come together for Steve. The Defender and Reason Lad had been in several of the newspaper clippings and photographs in Mr Hunter's basement, but who were the other costumed people pictured?

"Why did you decide to become superheroes? You're not going to tell me the town was crawling with supervillains."

Mr Hunter had a far-off look in his eyes as he reminisced. "You'd be surprised! I hadn't heard of any before we gained our powers, but in the following weeks all sorts of unsavoury characters began popping up. The Mischief Maker and his dastardly schemes, Madam Mesmera and her hypnotic ways, the Dancing Fool and his melody of doom – before we knew it the town was crawling with villains."

"Where did they come from?" asked Steve. "Was there some kind of evil laundry producing magic socks?"

"Billy and I used to discuss the very same thing," mused Mr Hunter. "It certainly seemed a coincidence that they appeared soon after we had discovered our own powers. When the Police struggled to cope we knew what we had to do: use our powers for the benefit of mankind."

"Okay, I guess I can see that. But why the costumes and the secret lair? If people knew and trusted you as a teacher, wouldn't it have been easier to let them know who you were?"

Steve considered this a perfectly reasonable question, which made Mr Hunter's reaction all the more surprising. The nostalgic look on his face was replaced with one of embarrassment as he studiously avoided Steve's gaze. "Yes, I suppose it might have been but I was trying to do right by Billy."

"Billy?" Steve interrupted, confused. "How so?"

"Because if I hadn't kept him back after class then he wouldn't have had his life changed by these powers. I wanted to help him adjust so I tracked down every superhero comic that I could lay my hands on. It was pretty clear from them that all superheroes needed a costume, a code name and a secret lair."

"Well that explains your tripped-out basement," mused Steve. "What about all your freaky gadgets?"

"I told you that I could come up with inventions to help us fight crime. And whenever we defeated a villain we would always confiscate their weapons and bring them back for safekeeping."

Steve burst out laughing. "Safekeeping? Yeah, you might have invested in some locked cases, I don't think that Pete particularly enjoyed being turned into a badger."

"A badger, eh?" Mr Hunter stroked his chin and looked quizzical, then he snapped his fingers and exclaimed, "EUREKA!

"This object that he touched: was it a green broach? I bet it was! We confiscated that from Anne E

Mal. She was obsessed with animals and thought they had to be protected from humans. She had a mad plan to turn everyone into badgers for some reason. Glad we stopped that one in time."

Steve listened in amazement as Mr Hunter rambled on about his past adventures, trying to make sense of all that he was hearing. It was the most exciting, craziest, out of this world story that he had ever heard, and he wanted it to be true with all of his heart. Superheroes and supervillains in his sleepy little town!

But where were all these supervillains? Where were the bank robberies and crazy schemes? The biggest crime that he could remember hitting Bridgeton was when someone had put a traffic cone on the statue outside the library.

Mr Hunter eventually noticed Steve's silence and broke off from his story. "What's the matter, Steven? You do believe me, don't you?"

Steve wrung his hands in frustration. "I want to, I really do! But there's so much that doesn't make sense. You say you're a superhero but I only know you as a mean old man. You say you were a teacher at my school but I've never heard you mentioned there. You don't even seem very sure what powers you're supposed to have!"

Mr Hunter's eyes narrowed and he opened his mouth to protest. But then his face drooped, transformed into a mask of sadness, and he sank deeper into his chair. Sprawled there and gazing up at the ceiling, he suddenly looked very tired, the youthful spark of his superhero transformation now faded.

"'I'm frustrated as well, you know. I've lost my job, my friends, my partner, my powers." He raised his hand and touched his cheek, tracing the deep wrinkles embedded there. "It feels like I've gone to sleep and woken up as an old man."

There was such sadness in his voice that Steve couldn't help feeling sorry for him, despite the bad blood between them in the past. "It might not be that bad, Mr Hunter. Maybe we can find Billy – do you remember what happened to him?"

"I hate to think," sighed Mr Hunter. "I know Billy, and if I was missing he wouldn't rest until he found out what had happened to me. Since he hasn't, I have to presume that he's not in Bridgeton anymore."

"Unless something wiped his memories as well," suggested Steve.

Mr Hunter froze, staring at Steve with his eyes bulging wide. Then a grin appeared on his face, spreading until it ran from ear to ear, and he jumped out of his chair like a cork exploding from a bottle.

"Of course, my boy, that must be it! I bet Billy's as ignorant as I was. Why, he'll be an adult by now – who knows where he's ended up. He could be a doctor, a mechanic, a –"

"Mr Hunter?"

Steve watched in concern as Mr Hunter stopped in mid-sentence, his mouth hanging open and his gaze fixed on the kitchen wall. For a second Steve worried that he was going to revert back to his grumpy old personality and he took a step back.

Instead Mr Hunter walked forward, reaching out and grabbing the calendar that was hanging on the wall. Produced by the school to raise funds, it featured photographs of all current pupils and staff.

It was the staff picture that Mr Hunter was focused on as he gazed intently at the smartly dressed teachers smiling for the camera.

Steve looked over his shoulder, the sight of his teachers reminding him that he was uncomfortably late for school. "What is it? What's the matter?"

Mr Hunter stretched out a finger and pointed to one of the teachers.

"That's him. A lot older than when I last saw him, but I'd know him anywhere. He's still there. He's still at the school."

"Who's at the school? What do you mean?"

Mr Hunter's eyes were still locked on the picture as he sank down into his seat.

"Billy," he breathed. "This man is Billy."

Steve looked at where Mr Hunter was pointing. At the man he had identified as Billy, also known as the superhero sidekick called Reason Lad.

Better known to Steve as his headteacher, Mr Spence.

11

OFFICIAL SUPERHERO BUSINESS

"We have to go! We have to go right now!"

Mr Hunter's eyes were alive with excitement as he pulled the calendar off the wall, holding it tightly. "I have to see Billy," he told Steve. "I have to remind him of who he is!"

"Woah, woah, woah – let's just slow down a second! Are you really saying that my headteacher used to be a superhero sidekick?"

"Only the very best one," replied Mr Hunter proudly. "That boy saved me on so many occasions – it's time I returned the favour!"

There was a sense of purpose about Mr Hunter that had been lacking only minutes before, all trace of self-pity now gone. "Are you coming?" he asked Steve.

Steve hesitated. It seemed unbelievable that Mr Spence had once been a superhero. He was quite a nice guy for a headteacher, but he just seemed so *normal*.

Although half an hour ago Mr Hunter had just been a grumpy old man and now he was... well, Steve wasn't quite sure what he was yet, but he knew that he should probably keep an eye on him.

He grabbed his schoolbag and ran after Mr Hunter, pulling the front door closed behind him.

They had almost reached the end of the garden when Mr Hunter stopped dead in his tracks, almost tripping Steve up.

"Mr Hunter, come on," he urged. "The bus we need to get stops on the next street."

"Oh, there's no time for buses, Steven. Time is of the essence, we'll have to fly there."

"Fly there," repeated Steve, staring at Mr Hunter

93

and wondering if he had heard him correctly. "You mean both of us?"

"Don't be silly," chided Mr Hunter. "You can't fly, I'll have to carry you. Now if I can just remember how to get things started."

He lifted his arms to the sky and tilted his head upwards, a look of intense concentration on his face.

His feet remained planted on the ground.

"Up, up and away," he shouted, hopping into the air.

He came straight back down again.

"Mr Hunter," interrupted Steve. "We can get the bus, I really don't mind."

Mr Hunter shushed him and crouched down. Then, like a coiled spring, he jumped up and started to run across the garden. He leapt into the air, arms outstretched, and for a moment he was suspended in mid-air...

Before crashing down to the ground with a loud thud that made Steve wince.

"Mr Hunter!" he shouted, running over to check on him. "Are you okay?"

Mr Hunter gingerly sat up and rubbed his shoulder, grimacing with discomfort. "A bit embarrassing to admit this, but I'm afraid that I've forgotten how to fly. We'll have to drive."

Steve looked at him in surprise. "Oh, okay. I didn't think you had a car."

Mr Hunter smiled and tapped his nose, appearing totally unconcerned. "I don't, but that's not a problem. We'll just borrow your mother's."

"You'll do *what?*" shrieked Steve. "You can't just borrow someone's car without asking them! You need their permission, and insurance, and probably to not be a crazy old man."

"I'll pretend I didn't hear that last part," sniffed Mr Hunter. "I know this is a lot to ask of you but time really is of the essence. Who knows what dastardly fiend wiped our memories, and for what sinister purpose."

He placed a hand on Steve's shoulder, looking into his eyes. "Every second that Billy doesn't remember who he is could be another second that he's in danger. Please, son, I wouldn't ask if it wasn't important."

Steve bit his lip and thought very hard about what to do next. Was a wrong still wrong if you were doing it to make something right? And if a right still felt wrong, was that because you weren't doing it right or because it really was wrong?

When it came down to it, he just didn't know. But he eventually decided that when in doubt, taking the option that could help people seemed like a good choice to make.

"Well... okay then," he sighed, unable to resist Mr Hunter's pleas. "I'll get the keys, but you have to *promise* to be careful!"

A few minutes later the two of them were sat inside his Mum's small Ford. Mr Hunter sat in the driver's seat, looking in amazement at the array of switches and buttons that filled the dashboard.

"Mr Hunter, you do know how to drive a car, don't you?" asked Steve, nervously checking his seatbelt for the eighth time.

"Of course I do. There are a few more bells and whistles than the last time I drove, but the basic principles are the same. Turn the key, handbrake off and pedal dow- **WOAH!**"

The car shot out of the drive like a bullet from a gun, narrowly missing a lamppost, and scaring a passing cat out of three of its nine lives. Steve grabbed the steering wheel and yanked it hard, just in time to stop an oak tree bringing their journey to a most untimely end.

Mr Hunter slammed on the brakes and the car came to a juddering halt, leaving its two passengers trying to catch their breath. Steve's stomach was doing backflips and his heart felt like it was trying to escape his chest.

"Mr Hunter, I'm not trying to be cheeky but are you absolutely sure that you can drive this car?"

Mr Hunter gave Steve a reassuring smile and patted the steering wheel, appearing totally unconcerned by their near miss. "The engine's a bit more powerful than I'm used to but don't worry, I can handle it."

He put the car into gear and they resumed their journey, pulling out of Bridge street and heading towards the centre of town. Mr Hunter initially kept the speed low but as his confidence grew it slowly crept up, causing Steve to tighten his grip on the car door.

As they entered the town centre they came to a zebra crossing. Steve watched as an old lady stepped onto the road, pulling her laden shopping trolley behind her.

Fixated on getting to the school as quickly as possible, Mr Hunter didn't notice her. He drove straight through the zebra crossing, forcing the woman to leap for safety with an impressive effort that would surely have won a gold medal in the pensioner long-jump category. Shopping spilled everywhere, with red apples and cans of beans rolling all over the road.

Mr Hunter stopped the car at the side of the road and looked in the rear-view mirror at the woman struggling to gather up her runaway goods.

"Look what you've done!" shouted Steve. "I know you're in a hurry but you've got to be more careful!"

"Don't worry, Steven," Mr Hunter reassured him. "I

know just how to fix this." He rolled down the driver's window and shouted to the old lady.

"Sorry about that, my dear. Afraid we can't stop – we're on official superhero business!"

Mr Hunter rolled up the window and started the car, before noticing Steve staring at him in slack-jawed amazement.

"What do you think you're doing?" Steve spluttered. "You can't tell anyone that you're a superhero – that's not how it works at all!"

Mr Hunter looked thoughtful, considering the wisdom of Steve's words. "Hmm, I suppose you're right. Sorry my boy, I'm a bit out of practice at this."

He put the car into reverse and drove backwards at speed. The old woman had almost finished picking up her shopping when she looked up and noticed the car bearing down on her. With a shriek of terror she dived out of the way as Mr Hunter screeched to a halt, knocking over the shopping trolley once more.

"Just to be clear, miss. I am not a superhero. Nope, definitely not. 100% normal, that's me!" Mr Hunter gave the woman a reassuring smile and tipped an imaginary hat. Then he drove off once again, visibly pleased with himself.

"There you go, my boy. All sorted."

He looked in the rear-view mirror and smiled. "Oh, how nice – she's waving at us."

Steve looked over his shoulder and saw the woman hopping from foot to foot, waving her arms about and looking very unhappy. She rolled up her sleeves and gathered up some of the now badly bruised apples.

"Um, I don't think she's waving," replied Steve, hunkering down in his seat so that no one else could see him.

The car continued its journey towards school, narrowly avoiding the barrage of apples launched in its direction from behind.

12

MEET GRANDAD

Mr Hunter pulled the car into a parking space and turned off the engine. He unbuckled his seatbelt and stepped out of the car, his eyes locked on the entrance to the school.

Steve stumbled out of the car and staggered over to join him, his stomach still doing backflips. "Are you okay?" he wheezed, trying his best not to bring up his breakfast.

"I'm not sure," replied Mr Hunter, not taking his eyes from the school. "In some ways being here seems so familiar, but it's been so long that I wonder if I belong anymore."

"Don't worry, no one feels like they belong in school," joked Steve, trying to make light of the situation. But when he saw the sadness in Mr Hunter's eyes he quickly realised that something more than jokes was required.

"I know it must be awful, but if you're right and you and Mr Spence both lost your memories then maybe the two of you can work out what to do next."

Mr Hunter nodded his head vigorously, the sadness in his gaze replaced by new determination. "You're right, my boy. Let's do this!" He marched towards the front door and Steve was forced to run in order to keep up with him.

Mr Hunter was about to press the buzzer when Steve stepped in front of him. "You better let me do the talking," he explained. "A lot of things have probably changed since you were last here."

He pressed the buzzer and after a few seconds they heard the soft click of the door being unlocked. Steve pushed open the door and walked inside, Mr Hunter following closely behind.

Steve was relieved to see that the reception area was empty apart from the bored looking secretary peering out from behind the glass panel – the last thing he wanted was for any of his friends to see him and start asking awkward questions.

As Mr Hunter was still looking around in amazement, Steve took charge of the situation. "Morning, Miss Albert," he smiled. "Sorry I'm late."

"You're very late," she replied, peering over the top of her dark glasses. "I hope you have a good excuse for this – no-one phoned to say that you'd be delayed."

"Oh yes, there's a very good reason – I had a stomach ac-"

"He had an exploding bottom."

Steve looked at Mr Hunter in horror, hardly able to believe what he'd just heard. Miss Albert didn't betray a flicker of emotion. "So, what was it? A stomach ache or an exploding bottom?"

"Erm, it was both actually," replied Steve, cringing with embarrassment. "It must have been something I ate. Maybe a bad egg or something."

"I see..." Miss Albert chewed the bottom of her pen and then gestured towards Mr Hunter. "And who's this you've brought with you? Your personal chef?"

Steve laughed nervously. "No, no – this is my unc-"

"I'm his granddad."

Mr Hunter smiled and gave Steve a thumbs up, completely oblivious to the dirty look he was giving him.

"Uh huh. So, tell me," asked Miss Albert, addressing Mr Hunter. "What is it? Are you his uncle or his grandad?"

"My uncle?" laughed Steve awkwardly. "No, I was going to say that he's my uncle's father."

"In other words, he's your grandad," replied Miss Albert, giving him a withering look. "Why on earth didn't you just say that?"

Mr Hunter opened his mouth to join the conversation but Steve jumped in front of him, cutting him off. "Excuse us a second," he called to Miss Albert. "I just need to have a quick word with gramps about something."

Without waiting for a reply Steve ushered Mr

Hunter into the corner of the room, as far away from Miss Albert as possible. "What are you doing?" he hissed. "I thought we'd agreed that I was going to do the talking."

"I was just trying to help," replied Mr Hunter, sounding a little hurt. "It would look pretty strange if your grandfather brought you to school and didn't say anything."

"You're not my –". Steve closed his eyes and counted to ten. "Mr Hunter, please just let me do the talking from now on. Thanks to you she thinks that my bottom exploded and that I come from a really weird family. I hate to think what you might say next."

"Alright, fine," pouted Mr Hunter. "As long as it helps us get close to Billy."

"Grandad," Miss Albert called from the other side of the room, her voice dripping with sarcasm. "Come over here, please."

Steve shook his head furiously but Mr Hunter didn't take the hint. "Trust me," he whispered to Steve, giving him an exaggerated wink as he walked over to Miss Albert.

She looked Mr Hunter up and down, obviously trying to make her mind up about the mysterious individual in front of her. "So, you're Steven's grandad?" she asked.

"That's right," beamed Mr Hunter.

"Lovely," smiled Miss Albert, and for a moment Steve relaxed. Then she hit Mr Hunter with a sucker punch. "If you're Steven's grandad then I'm sure you can tell me what his surname is," she said, smiling sweetly.

This seemed a perfectly straightforward question, but when Steve saw the panicked look on Mr Hunter's face he realised to his horror that there were still gaps in the old man's memory.

"Why, of course I can," replied Mr Hunter, chuckling nervously. "I am his grandad after all. It's erm... that is, erm..." His eyes darted towards Steve, desperately hunting for a clue.

Steve stepped backwards so that he was out of Miss Albert's line of sight. He tapped his ear and then held out his palm, running his fingers along the top as if they were marching from side to side.

Mr Hunter looked at him in confusion and Steve groaned with frustration. Dropping to his knees he marched his fingers across the floor. Then he took his thumb and his forefinger and held them very close together, until they were almost touching.

"Sounds like ant," Mr Hunter muttered.

"His name's Steven Plant!" he announced confidently.

Miss Albert's reply was drowned out by the sound of Steve coughing loudly. He held up his hands in front of him as if they were monstrous paws, before pulling his face into a fearsome snarl.

"Growl! Steven Growl," announced Mr Hunter, certain that he'd finally got there.

Steve coughed again and Miss Albert leaned forward in an attempt to see what he was doing.

"Steven Bark! No, Steven Snarl! No, Steven Grr!"

Mr Hunter paused and Steve could almost see the lightbulb switch on above his head.

"Steven Grrrant" he exclaimed in delight. "His name's Steven Grant."

Steve came forward to join Mr Hunter at the

reception window, pretending not to notice Miss Albert's look of displeasure. "Sorry about grandad," he told her. "He's not as funny as he likes to think he is."

Miss Albert sniffed with irritation. "He's certainly not, it must run in the family." She turned away from them and back to her computer. "Thank you for bringing Steven in, Sir. Goodbye now."

"Wait!" interrupted Mr Hunter. "I'd actually like to see Billy if that's okay?"

"Billy?" Miss Albert asked. "If Steven wants to see his little friends then he can wait until after school."

"He means Mr Spence," Steve clarified. "Can me and grandad see him? It's really important."

Miss Albert gave an exaggerated sigh and picked up the telephone. She quickly keyed a number as Steve and Mr Hunter exchanged glances, hoping that their luck would hold out.

"Mr Spence?... Yes, it's Miss Albert here. I have a pupil and his carer who would like to see you – is this a good time?... Marvellous, I'll send them on. Thank you. Bye."

Miss Albert hung up the phone and pressed a

switch underneath her desk, causing the school's interior doors to swing open. "You can go through to his office now but don't be long, he's very busy."

Steve and Mr Hunter hurried through before she changed her mind. The doors swung closed behind them, but not before a passer-by had spotted them.

Dinner lady Mary had returned from picking up extra mince just in time to catch sight of Steve and Mr Hunter. She stood stock still with the strangest expression on her face. It was a look of pure amazement and astonishment, the look of someone who has seen a ghost.

"It can't be," she muttered. "Not here, not now." Shaking her head in disbelief, she hurried off.

13

FRIENDS REUNITED

Steve led Mr Hunter along the corridor towards Mr Spence's office. Mr Hunter kept gazing around him in astonishment, remarking on all the things that had changed since he had last been at the school, and Steve had to constantly prod him onwards.

When they arrived at the office, Mr Hunter bent forward to examine the brass nameplate on the door. It read: *Mr Spence: Headteacher*.

"Oh, Billy," he whispered. "You've done so well for yourself."

Steve shuffled his feet, feeling like he was intruding

on a private moment. It almost looked like Mr Hunter was about to start crying, and that was the last thing he wanted. Taking evasive action, he reached out and knocked firmly on the closed door. "Come in," shouted a voice from inside.

Mr Hunter gripped the door handle and, after a moment's hesitation, pushed open the door and walked inside. Steve followed, pulling the door closed behind him.

Mr Spence was on the phone, his chair turned to look out of the window. He briefly looked round and motioned for Mr Hunter and Steve to take a seat, before returning his attention to the call.

"So, we're agreed then – we'll get the equipment for 10% less than the catalogue price? ... Excellent, that's great... No, thank you." He hung up the phone and turned to them with a look of quiet satisfaction on his face.

"Sorry about that, gentlemen, just finalising a little business with some suppliers. A headteacher's work is never done!"

He chuckled at his own joke and then looked

curiously at Mr Hunter, who was staring at him in barely-disguised amazement. Mr Spence extended his hand and shook Mr Hunter's. "Good morning, Sir, I don't believe we've met. I'm Mr Spence, and you are?"

"He's my grandad," Steve interrupted. "He brought me to school because I wasn't feeling well earlier."

"Ah, thank you, Mr Grant. Good of you to make sure Steve got here okay. A grandad's work is never done, eh? Was there something else that I can do for you?"

Mr Hunter didn't answer. He just sat looking at Mr Spence, staring at him intently.

Mr Spence turned a little pale, obviously beginning to wonder exactly what kind of crazy person he had let into his office. "Mr Grant," he prompted. "Are you okay, Sir?"

Mr Hunter jumped to his feet, sending the chair he was sitting on crashing backwards. "I'm not Mr Grant," he announced. "And you're not Mr Spence!"

Steve tugged at his sleeve, trying to attract his attention. "Grandad, calm down. I thought we agreed we were going to play this cool."

"What do you mean I'm not Mr Spence? Who else would I be? And who are you?"

"I'm The Defender," declared Mr Hunter. "And you're Reason Lad. The two of us were the greatest superheroes this town has ever seen."

Mr Spence slowly backed away from them, his hand reaching out and fumbling for the phone on his desk. "I don't know what kind of silly joke this is, Mr Grant, but I really am very busy. I'll have to ask you to leave or I'm going to phone security."

"Phone security?" spluttered Mr Hunter. "But why? You know me, you just have to remember!" Then he saw the terrified look on Mr Spence's face and staggered backwards, with Steve having to support him.

"You really don't remember anything, do you?" he moaned. "You have no idea who I am."

"I'm sorry, Mr Grant, I really don't. Is there someone that you'd like me to call? You seem upset."

Too distraught to reply, Mr Hunter slumped against the wall in despair. As Steve looked at him an unusual feeling came over him. In the time that he'd known Mr Hunter he'd felt a variety of emotions – had been scared, annoyed and upset. But now, seeing how devastated he was, Steve only felt sorry for him.

"Mr Spence – Billy - you have to listen to him. You found a magic sock! You were superheroes! You have to remember that, even if no-one else does. Just think, please!"

"What did you call me?" Mr Spence looked at Steve in confusion. "What do you mean a magic sock?"

He was silent for a second, as if thinking hard, and for a moment Steve dared to hope that his plea had worked. But then Mr Spence shook his head and his expression of mild irritation returned. "I'm sorry but I'm going to have to ask you to leave. I'm very busy."

As if to prove his point, Mr Spence set about tidying up the scattered papers on his desk. He picked up one sheet and scanned its contents, before rolling it into a ball and throwing it towards the bin.

It hit the bin with a thud, causing it to rock back and forth.

Mr Spence looked at the bin and then at Steve and Mr Hunter, and it seemed as if a fog slowly lifted from his eyes. He came out from behind his desk and hurried over to the still despondent Mr Hunter. Then he threw his arms around him and gave him a big hug.

"It's good to see you again, Sir," he smiled.

***

"I still can't believe we're together again," chuckled Mr Hunter. "And now you're a headteacher! I'm so proud of you."

Mr Spence smiled modestly. "Well, it's not quite as exciting as protecting people from bad guys, but I like to think that I still do my bit for the town."

"Do you remember everything now?" interrupted Steve. "Do you know why you lost your memory?"

Mr Spence's brow furrowed with concentration as he considered his answer. "It's slowly coming back to me, yes. I remember getting my powers... I remember us fighting crime... but I have no idea what happened in the interim."

He turned to Mr Hunter. "I didn't even remember you when you walked in," he said apologetically, "and you were like a second father to me."

Mr Hunter placed a hand on his shoulder and gave a comforting squeeze. "No need to beat yourself up, Billy – I was exactly the same until young Steven here brought me to my senses. The important thing is that now we're together we can work out what happened to us."

"It's obvious," Steve chipped in. "It must have been one of your enemies. You fought lots of supervillains, could any of them have done this?"

Mr Hunter stroked his chin thoughtfully. "I don't recall any of them having the power to alter memories like this, but it's certainly a possibility. Someone obviously wanted us both out of the way."

"It's actually pretty weird when you think about it," Steve said. "You would think a supervillain would trap you in a volcano or bury you underground. Instead, you were turned into a grumpy old man and Mr Spence became a headteacher."

Mr Hunter chuckled. "Yes, I think I definitely came off worst in that deal. Still, it makes perfect sense when you think about it. If they wanted to keep me and Billy apart, what better way to do it then by making me someone who disliked children. Why, that would practically guarantee that I'd never set foot in here."

Steve swung back on his chair, trying to think things through. "Okay, I can see that. But if it was a supervillain plan to get rid of you both, what happened to all the supervillains? Surely they would have committed all sorts of crimes without you to stop them."

"Perhaps they didn't think it was a challenge without any heroes to fight," suggested Mr Spence. "Think about Batman – most of the time the Joker only commits crimes to get his attention."

Steve let Mr Hunter and Mr Spence talk, trying to work things through in his head. He couldn't help thinking that he was missing something – something obvious.

"It sounds like things were really bad for you," Mr Spence said to Mr Hunter. "I hope you haven't been too unhappy these past years."

"It almost feels like another me," Mr Hunter reassured him. "And I'm sure you've had your own complications. Why, I imagine if you'd remembered about your powers then it would have been pretty tempting to make some of the children change their ways. Turn a bully into a model citizen and all that."

He chortled and slapped Mr Spence on the back. "Not that you'd ever do that, of course!"

Steve's blood ran cold as a terrible thought occurred to him.

He frantically tugged at Mr Hunter's sleeve, trying to get his attention. "Mr Hunter, I need to talk to you – in private."

"Don't be so rude, Steven. Anything you have to say to me you can say in front of Billy here."

"It's okay," laughed Mr Spence. "Old habits die hard and Steve's known me as a headteacher for a lot longer than as a superhero. Take all the time you need."

Steve grabbed Mr Hunter's hand and pulled him towards the corner of the room. "Mr Hunter," he whispered. "You have to listen to me carefully, this is really important."

"Well, obviously," rebuked Mr Hunter. "I think you

almost pulled my arm out of its socket."

"I'm sorry, but just listen to me. Someone made you forget who you were. Someone didn't want you coming to the school and meeting Mr Spence. Think about it – who would have the power to make you do that?"

Mr Hunter looked at him curiously. "I'm sorry, but you've lost me. That's exactly what we've been trying to find out."

"Mr Spence – Billy!" Steve hissed. "You've said yourself that he could talk people into doing anything he said. Like convincing you that you're not a superhero! Like making you think there's no door in your hallway!"

Mr Hunter roughly pulled his arm away, his annoyance evident. "How *dare* you say that! I've known Billy for years – he's a good person. Why on earth would he do something like this?"

"I don't know," replied Steve, "but at least keep it in mind, please."

Mr Hunter's reply was cut off by the sound of clapping. Steve turned around and saw Mr Spence standing in front of his desk, applauding.

"Young Steven, you never do know when to keep quiet, do you?"

"Mr Hunter," whispered Steve urgently. "I think we should go!"

"Both of you – come here and sit down. Now!"

Steve tried to resist but it was as if some other force was controlling his legs. No matter how he tried to direct them towards the door they just kept walking forward, before depositing him down in the seat. In no time at all he and Mr Hunter found themselves sitting before Mr Spence, unable to move.

"Billy," Mr Hunter spluttered in confusion. "What's the meaning of this?"

Mr Spence smiled, but there was nothing reassuring about it at all. It reminded Steve of the kind of smile an owl might give a mouse shortly before gobbling it up.

"Sit still and listen, 'old friend'. I think it's long overdue that we had a proper catch up."

14

MEMORIES ARE MADE OF THIS

In some ways, the situation felt quite familiar.

Steve had been sent to Mr Spence's office many times before and had sat in the same uncomfortable red seat opposite the cluttered desk. It was always covered with paperwork, pens and assorted folders, with Mr Spence sitting behind it dispensing his latest words of wisdom.

Steve sat in the same chair and the desk was covered with the same clutter, but there was one important difference. He wasn't normally held captive by a headteacher who had turned out to be a supervillain.

Steve moved Mr Spence down a few places in his mental ranking of the school's teachers, leaving him level-last with Mary. Steve didn't think that she was a supervillain, but her cooking was certainly a deadly weapon.

"Billy! Why are you doing this? What's going on?"

Mr Hunter's face was bright red and Steve could clearly see the throbbing veins on his forehead. Steve guessed that Mr Hunter was encountering the same problem he had: that no matter how hard he tried he couldn't get up from his chair.

"You really don't have a clue, do you?" sneered Mr Spence. "You may be older now but you're definitely not any smarter."

"Leave him alone!" shouted Steve, "You're meant to be his friend! Why are you doing this?"

Mr Spence didn't answer. Appearing totally unconcerned by Steve's accusations, he moved some papers to one side and sat down on his desk. "Don't say a word," he warned, before picking up the phone and dialling.

"Miss Albert... if you could just hold my calls, please, I'm in an important meeting... Yes, I'll let you know when I'm finished."

Steve tried to shout or make a noise. "I'm here!" he wanted to scream. "Help us!" But as hard as he tried – no matter how loud he shouted within his head – no sound escaped his lips.

Mr Spence hung up the phone and turned to face them. "You never do know when to keep quiet, do you Steven?" He waited for a response, before chuckling as he realised his mistake. "Speak," he said.

"This has gone far enough," chided Mr Hunter. "Billy, stop these silly games and explain what on earth you're doing."

Mr Spence slid off the desk and walked up to Mr Hunter's chair, before crouching down and looking him in the eye. "Billy is a name for a silly little child; my name is William. And as for what I'm doing, I'll tell you. Someone should know after all these years."

"What has he told you?" he asked Steve. "Let me guess – we were the best of chums who spent our days at school, our nights fighting crime and our weekends doing as many good deeds as possible."

"Something like that," muttered Steve, trying to ignore the hurt look on Mr Hunter's face.

"Well here's something that he probably didn't mention. He wouldn't let us get any payment for helping people. He wouldn't even let us get money from sponsorship deals or interviews. He said that wasn't the way heroes behaved. All that work and what did I get out of it?"

"You helped people," replied a confused Mr Hunter. "People who couldn't help themselves! What more could you want?"

"I wanted what was owed me," snapped Mr Spence. "I received these amazing powers and you made me hide them away behind a mask. I could have been rich and famous."

"You loved superheroes!" protested Mr Hunter. "And I know you liked helping people. What we did for this town was important – we kept people safe."

"Exactly!" shouted Mr Spence, throwing his arms wide and sending papers and reports flying. "We kept them safe and what did we get in return? Absolutely nothing."

"You never said you were unhappy. Why didn't you tell me?"

Mr Spence fell silent and looked away, briefly unable to hold Mr Hunter's gaze. Realisation dawned for Steve.

"Mr Hunter, I think he did."

Mr Spence nodded, and Steve thought he saw a flicker of guilt that vanished almost as soon as it appeared.

"I did, once, and you told me that we didn't have these powers for our benefit but to help other people. And so I made you forget that we'd talked about it. That's when I first realised how much easier life would be if I started using my powers to help me."

"Oh, Billy," whispered Mr Hunter. "Please tell me you didn't."

"You never wondered where all the supervillains went, did you? You were just happy that they weren't a problem anymore, but that was only thanks to me. One by one I made them forget who they were, making them think they were just ordinary men and women."

Steve could hardly believe what he was hearing. "You made them forget who they were? That's evil, you can't do that!"

Mr Spence smiled. "Oh, is it now? Even though making them forget helped keep the whole town safe?"

"Yes, it is," replied Mr Hunter without hesitation. "We kept people safe, Billy. It wasn't our job to decide how the bad guys should be punished."

BANG!

Mr Spence pounded his fist on the desk, knocking over a plastic cup and sending a tiny river of tea sailing along.

"You never change, you always think you know best. That's why after the supervillains the next thing I had to do was take care of you."

For a moment there was silence in the room. From the other side of the window Steve could hear the distant rumble of traffic and occasional birdsong. It all seemed so ordinary compared to the crazy scene he found himself in.

Mr Spence moved closer to Mr Hunter, who stared back without flinching. He was trying to look stern and disapproving but Steve could see that his eyes were moist and knew that he must be hurting terribly.

"I knew that even if there were no supervillains you would still want us to do good deeds for the town. That's when I decided that I'd have to make you forget, too."

"Make me forget," repeated Mr Hunter in disbelief. Then his face darkened as realization dawned. "It was you!" he shouted. "How could you do that to me?"

"It was easy, really," replied Mr Spence. "All I had to do was convince you that you were an ordinary man who found children annoying and wanted to be left alone. Oh, and I couldn't have you discovering all the goodies in your basement so I made you forget it even existed."

Mr Hunter sank deeper into his chair in stunned silence, his faith in his old friend finally shattered. Steve's heart ached for him. Could there be anything worse than finding out that your best friend was responsible for the worst thing to ever happen to you? Suddenly Peter breaking a few toys didn't seem quite as important.

"I get why you told him to be an ordinary man and to forget the basement," Steve interrupted, "but why did you tell him he found children annoying?"

"Ahh, well that was clever of me," smiled Mr Spence. "I knew that if I kept him away from familiar locations then there would be less chance of his memory returning. And, of course, it meant that I could finish my education without fear of discovery."

"You're a monster," shouted Steve, feeling angrier than he had ever been before. "You took away everything he knew, just so you could have an easier life? He was your friend!"

Mr Spence's eyes flicked towards Mr Hunter, who was slumped in his chair and looking utterly defeated.

"I deserved it," he protested. "What's the point in helping everyone but yourself?"

Steve's head hurt. This was his headteacher saying these things – the same man who had given him countless lectures on acceptable behaviour within the classroom. Not for the first time that day he found himself wishing that this was all just a really bizarre dream.

Thinking carefully, he tried to reason out what he'd learned.

"Okay, so you didn't have to be a superhero and you could use your powers to help you in life. So why become a headteacher and stay at this school? If you could get anything you wanted, wouldn't you rather be somewhere more exciting than Bridgeton?"

"It's because you loved the school and wanted to help children, isn't it, Billy?" Mr Hunter interrupted. "No matter what you've done to me, I know that you're a good person really."

Mr Spence turned away and looked out of the window, as if gathering his thoughts. When he replied his voice was low, with none of the swaggering confidence it had possessed only minutes ago.

"Do you know what school was like for me? Oh, I may have been clever and achieved good grades, but I was never close to the other children. And it became worse after I got powers – it was yet another thing that set me apart.

"But do you know what happens now I'm a headteacher? The same boys and girls that never had time for me when they were younger, now they come in with their own children. And I shake their hands and I invite them into my office for a chat. And I persuade them to give me whatever they can – money, jewellery, watches – before making them forget all about it."

"That's horrible," Steve gasped. Then he remembered his Mum searching the house for her favourite ring, right after she had come to the school for parents' evening. Just how many things had Mr Spence stolen over the years?

"You're a disgrace!" shouted Mr Hunter, his beaten expression replaced by hot anger. "These people have done nothing to you and you take from them like a common thief!" He rocked back and forward with all of his might, causing his chair to wobble from side to side.

"Make all the fuss you want," soothed Mr Spence. "You'll soon forget this, then you can return to that little house of yours and things can go back to normal."

Mr Hunter didn't rise to the bait and continued to rock back and forward. Then, when his chair was leaning precariously to one side, he pushed out his leg and kicked it off the desk. His chair toppled over and slammed into Steve's, knocking it to the ground.

The two of them lay on the floor, still rooted to their chairs at Mr Spence's command, unable to break free.

"Oh, do get up," he fumed, and Steve and Mr Hunter slowly rose to their feet. Then, before Mr Spence could say anything else, Mr Hunter jumped towards him, pushing him down onto the desk.

"Run, boy," he shouted at Steve. "Get help!"

Steve ran to the door and yanked it open, while behind him an angry Mr Spence threw Mr Hunter aside. He pointed a finger at Steve and opened his mouth to issue a command.

BRIIIIING

The school bell drowned out all other noise. Although Steve could see Mr Spence's lips moving he could hear no words. Throwing himself out the door he slammed it behind him and dashed down the corridor as fast as he could.

By the time that the last echo of the bell had faded away, Steve was out of sight on a desperate mission to find help.

15

ROUND UP THE GANG

Steve ran down the corridor at full speed, trying to put as much distance between himself and Mr Spence as possible. He felt terrible for leaving Mr Hunter behind and hated to think what was going to happen to him, but at least he was free to get help.

There was just one *tiny* little problem. He had no idea where to go for help, or who he could trust. The police would think he was playing a prank if he phoned to report that his headteacher was a supervillain. And as for the other teachers in school, what if they had already been brainwashed by Mr

Spence?

Steve hurtled around a corner into the main section of the school and came to an abrupt stop. The corridor was quickly filling up as pupils poured out of their classrooms, heading towards the canteen. Some recognised Steve and shouted greetings, but most were too caught up in their own conversations to notice him or wonder why he was so out of breath.

"Steven Grant!"

A familiar voice called from behind and Steve tensed, ready to run. He warily turned around and saw Mrs Baxter striding towards him, looking as grumpy as ever.

"Steven. What is the meaning of this? You're not in my class all morning and now I find you running through the corridors like a boy possessed. Would you care to explain yourself?"

Steve quickly weighed up whether to tell Mrs Baxter the truth. She was a bit of a battleaxe, but seemed quite a decent person and might be willing to help. The only problem was that she had the imagination of a turnip. A particularly stupid turnip.

No, it was too risky to confide in Mrs Baxter.

"Sorry, Mrs Baxter. I wasn't feeling well this morning and now that I'm here I don't want to be late for lunch and miss out on all the food."

Mrs Baxter looked at him in surprise, one eyebrow slightly raised. "You actually want to eat the food in the canteen?"

"Oh yes, it's delicious," Steve replied, hoping that Mrs Baxter took him at his word. If she subjected him to a taste test then there was no way that he could keep up the pretence.

"I think you're still a little sick, Steven – possibly delusional. Enjoy your lunch." Mrs Baxter walked past him and continued along the corridor, shouting out instructions and rebukes to pupils as she went.

Hoping that his luck would hold, Steve set off for the canteen. He might not want to try the food but his conversation with Mrs Baxter had given him an idea for someone who might be able to help.

***

Steve burst through the double doors of the canteen, the swinging doors knocking the lunch tray from a passing student's hands. Her lunch shot into the air, showering her with orange juice and mince from head to toe and leaving the poor girl a sticky mess.

"Sorry!" Steve apologised as he hurried past, his eyes scanning the room. The canteen was noisy, the air filled with the laughter of children, the clink of crockery and the scaping of cutlery. The pupils with packed lunches looked the happiest as they tucked into their sandwiches, while their friends with school dinners forced down their mince with weary resignation.

Finally, Steve spotted Peter at a table in the centre of the room and ran over to join him. Peter didn't seem to be showing any ill-effects from his strange transformation. He was tucking into his mince with relish and was smiling happily as he listened to the person sitting next to him...

Jill Mckenzie????!

Steve couldn't believe his eyes. Of all the things to happen to him today, this was without doubt the strangest. Laughing and joking with his worst enemy? How could Peter do that?

That sneaky sneak!

That terrible traitor!

That bad badger!

Steve marched up to the table and sat down opposite Peter. Neither Peter nor Jill noticed, with both of them too engrossed in their conversation.

"AHEM!"

Steve cleared his throat loudly and Peter looked round, dropping his fork in surprise when he saw him.

"Steve, hi!" he stammered, instantly turning bright red. "I didn't realise you were here."

"Obviously not," replied Steve. "I hope that you haven't been too lonely without your BEST FRIEND."

Before Peter could answer, Jill cut in. "He's been just fine, thank you. Without you here he's been able to have a sensible conversation for once."

"More like you've been talking his ear off and he's too polite to tell you to go away," snorted Steve.

"I'll have you know that Peter enjoys our little chats very much."

"Oh, sure he does. Like someone enjoys going to the dentist."

"You're wrong, Steven. But then again, you're wrong about everything, aren't you?"

"Oh, I'm wrong am I? Let's see what Pete has to say about that!"

"Yes, let's!"

Jill and Steve turned to stare at Peter, who shrank down in his seat looking very uncomfortable.

"Um, well, the thing is... that is... um..." Scared of saying the wrong thing, Peter struggled to reply. Then he saw a chance to steer the conversation onto safer ground.

"How's Mr Hunter?" he asked Steve. "Did you get him back to his house okay?"

Steve's eyes boggled as he remembered why he'd come here in the first place. How could he have forgotten? "Pete, I need your help – Mr Spence is a supervillain!"

Peter stared at him in surprise, wondering whether this was one of Steve's jokes. "Mr Spence is a supervillain? Really?"

"Yes! Well, kind of. See, at first he was Reason Lad but then he became a bad guy and he mindwiped Mr

Hunter and now he's in his office and he's got Mr Hunter and he's being all evil and we've JUST GOT TO DO SOMETHING QUICKLY!"

Peter puckered his lips in concentration, his brow furrowing as he tried to take in all that he'd heard.

"Mr Spence was a superhero as well?"

"Yes!"

"But he wiped Mr Hunter's memories?"

"Yes!"

"And now he's... an evil headteacher?"

"Yes!"

"Our Mr Spence?"

"YES!"

Peter leaned back in his chair, biting his lip as he stared up at the ceiling. "Huh," he said, "that was unexpected."

Jill gave him a sharp jab in the ribs, almost making him fall off the chair. "Peter, don't tell me you believe any of that nonsense he's spouting. He just doesn't want us to sit together, that's all."

"It's all true," shouted Steve, desperately trying to convince her. "I thought my next-door neighbour was a grumpy old man, then I realised he was a supervillain but he's actually a superhero and Pete got turned into a badger and–"

"Wait, hold on." Jill looked at Peter in confusion. "You got turned into what?"

"A badger," replied Peter, examining his hands closely as if looking for proof. "It was not the best start to the day."

Jill folded her arms and looked at Peter crossly. "Peter Rennie, this is not funny. I expect this sort of nonsense from Steven but not from you."

"It's true you annoying know-it-all!" shouted Steve, growing increasingly frustrated. "And we have to do something before Mr Spence makes us forget what we've discovered!"

He pushed his chair back and climbed up on top of the table. A few curious heads turned towards him, wondering what he was doing, but the majority of the room were too involved in their own conversations to notice.

Steve took a deep breath, sucking in air until it felt like his lungs were about to pop.

"QUUUUUUUUIIIIIIIIIIIIIIIEEEEEEEEETTTTTTTT!"

he shouted, as loudly as he could.

Conversation stopped.

Cutlery was put down.

All eyes were on Steve.

Suddenly nervous at being the centre of attention, he swallowed and tried to calm his thumping heart.

"You all have to listen to me, this is really important!"

"Get down from there, boy," shouted Mary from the other side of the room.

"No, I have to tell you all about Mr Spence. You can't trust him, he-"

The school PA system crackled into life, drowning out Steve's plea. The soothing voice of Mr Spence filled the room.

"Good afternoon, I hope you are all enjoying your lunch. There is a troublemaker called Steven Grant currently loose in our school. If you find him you are to bring him to my office. I repeat, you are to bring him to my office. Thank you."

As Mr Spence's words faded away there was

silence, and Steve readied himself to continue his plea. Then he heard the scraping of a chair and he looked round to find Jenny Wishart standing up and pointing at him.

"There he is," she shouted. "Let's take him to the office."

All around the canteen, pupils abandoned their lunch and their conversations and stood up, their eyes fixed on Steve. They rose from their chairs came out from their tables and began to walk towards him. Steve could see that their eyes were glazed, almost like they were sleepwalking.

"Pete," he whispered. "I think we're in big trouble now."

There was no reply.

Steve looked round only to see Peter and Jill rising to their feet, the same blank expression on their faces.

"We have him," called Jill, dribbling slightly.

"We must take him to the office," droned Peter, staring at Steve with no hint of recognition.

The two reached towards Steve with outstretched arms while from all across the canteen hypnotised pupils marched towards him, eager to carry out Mr Spence's demands.

16

STEVE AGAINST THE WORLD

Brainwashed zombies to the left of him.

Brainwashed zombies to the right of him.

Brainwashed zombies all around him.

Steve tried his best to remain calm. It definitely looked bad, but surely he'd been in worse situations before?

There was a shrill clanging sound and Steve looked round to see Mary emerge from behind the counter, waving her serving ladle about her head and whacking it off walls.

Nope, Steve decided. *This is absolutely, positively,*

the worst situation that I've ever been in.

Pupils swarmed around the table from all directions, stretching out their arms to grab him. Steve retreated as far as he could until he was left standing in the middle of the table on one leg, wobbling precariously back and forward.

"Pete, come on," he pleaded, "it's me, Steve!"

Peter didn't reply and didn't even seem to hear his best friend. He continued to stretch out, his fingertips clawing at Steve's clothes.

Steve gulped. If he couldn't even manage to persuade Peter, what chance did he have of convincing anyone else?

"This has all been a really big mistake," he announced to the assembled crowd. "I'm the good guy here, it's Mr Spence that's the baddie."

"Mr Spence..." replied a small boy with fair hair, suddenly looking rather confused. Steve instantly perked up. Perhaps he was breaking through to people!

"Yes, Mr Spence, that's right," he encouraged him. The other pupils paused their efforts to capture Steve and turned to watch, their faces expressionless.

"Mr Spence..." repeated the boy, before smiling with the joy of discovery. "Mr Spence wants us to take you to his office," he announced proudly.

The crowd cheered and immediately resumed their pursuit.

Steve groaned. What he wouldn't give for a helping hand right now. Anyone would do, even an offer of help from Jill Mckenzie would be gratefully received at this stage.

He thrust his hands into his trouser pockets, frantically searching for something that could help him escape. A smoke bomb; a catapult; a pencil sharpener – anything at all!

Steve's search didn't reveal anything of note but when he braved a look back at his pursuers he noticed that they were now further away.

Steve blinked in confusion. Were they retreating? Had Mr Spence made another announcement that he'd missed?

Then he noticed something very odd. Peter and Jill were still at the front of the crowd, pressed up against the table he was standing on. Yet they definitely seemed further away – what on earth was going on?

Steve looked down and saw something so crazy, so mind bogglingly strange, that at first his brain simply refused to believe it. And Steve had already seen his best friend turned into a badger that day, so his tolerance for weirdness was pretty high.

The crazy sight was the fact that he was no longer standing on the table.

To be precise he was now floating *above* the table, suspended in mid-air.

Steve closed his eyes and counted to five.

He opened them again and looked down.

Yep, he was still floating.

Steve checked to see whether he had grown wings. He thought it rather unlikely, but then again it had been that kind of day.

Nope, no wings.

Very carefully, he took one leg and waved it around, first from side-to-side and then up and down. He didn't make contact with anything, so ruled out an invisible support.

It was shaping up to be a good news/bad news situation.

In the good news category, he appeared to be flying. True, it wasn't the best of circumstances to make that discovery, but it was still undeniably awesome. It also had the happy effect of keeping him out of his classmates' clutches.

In the bad news category, he seemed to be stuck in mid-air, as if caught in an invisible spider's web. He might be safe for the moment but the fact that Mr Spence could capture him by using a small stepladder didn't suggest this was a viable solution in the long-term.

Then Steve noticed something. On his finger was the ring that he had found in Mr Hunter's basement, which had been in his pocket and forgotten about ever since.

Steve held his hand up in front of his face and wiggled his fingers, examining the ring closely. It looked perfectly normal, could it really have anything to do with him flying? Remembering some of the other strange gadgets in Mr Hunter's basement, Steve supposed it was at least possible.

He grasped the ring and slowly began to pull it off his finger. When it had almost reached his fingernail, Steve began to lose height and descend towards the table. He quickly slipped the ring back on and rose into the air once more.

Making doubly sure, he moved the ring up and down his finger several times. Eventually, after being repeatedly lowered and raised into the air, he felt rather queasy and decided that was more than enough testing.

It was the ring! Mr Hunter hadn't been able to fly because he had forgotten that he needed the ring!

Steve felt excitement building up within him – he had a chance to escape! But first he had to learn to control it. The last thing he wanted was to get outside and find that he kept flying higher and higher, on a one-way trip into space.

Steve could see no buttons or writing on the ring, leaving him none the wiser on how it worked. Then he remembered how he had floated upwards when he had first put it on, at the very moment he had been desperate to escape his classmates' clutches.

Did it read my mind? he wondered.

There was only one way to find out.

He pictured himself rising into the air and almost immediately found himself drifting up towards the ceiling. Laughing in disbelief, he thought about moving over to the canteen windows and within seconds he was flying over, past the heads of his brainwashed classmates who stared up at him in dull surprise.

"I'll come back for you," shouted Steve. "Don't worry, I'll fix this, I promise."

He pulled open the small upper window and squeezed through, trying not to notice how high up he was. With a final heave he was through and floating in mid-air outside the school walls. He pulled the window closed and allowed himself a small sigh of satisfaction.

There was just one problem remaining. What on earth was he going to do now?

17

UP, UP AND AWAY

Twenty minutes later, Steve finally arrived back at his house. His school uniform was torn and covered in stains and his hair looked like he had been dragged through a hedge backwards. He was also *exceedingly* smelly.

It had turned out that flying was not quite as fun as he'd imagined it would be.

It had started off okay – he had flown away from the school feeling as free as a bird, enjoying the feeling of the wind in his hair. Anxious to avoid being seen, he had flown high into the sky: high enough to avoid people, hopefully low enough to avoid planes.

Unfortunately, the birds weren't keen on sharing the sky with a ten-year-old schoolboy. He had heard the squawking of one bird, then another and another, until finally he was surrounded by birds, none of whom looked particularly pleased to see him.

The braver ones came closer, pecking at his clothes, while others remained above him and contented themselves with directing a constant barrage of bird poo in his direction.

After only a few minutes, Steve was sore, sticky, and altogether lost. If you've ever been on an aeroplane then you'll know how different even the most familiar sight can look from up in the sky. When your vision is obscured by angry seagulls and drips of bird poo, it's even harder to get your bearings.

"Get off," he shouted, waving his arms about. "I'm in a hurry, this is important!"

Unfortunately for Steve, seagulls don't speak English and so his pleading fell on deaf ears. Even if they did, they probably wouldn't have cared. Seagulls are the supervillains of the bird world.

Growing braver as they saw Steve's distress, more and more birds swooped towards him, causing him to wobble from side to side as he tried to avoid them. He was finding it increasingly hard to concentrate and felt himself slowly losing height.

Steve shielded his eyes and looked about him, trying

to find a familiar landmark. Where exactly was he? His eyes darted from side to side but nothing looked familiar and he decided to fly lower and work out where he was.

The birds spotted Steve descending and squawked in delight, sensing victory. They dived towards him in unison, making one final attempt to evict him from the sky.

Steve saw the approaching shadow and looked round just in time to see a colony of very angry seagulls diving towards him. He instantly had one overriding thought – he had to get back down to the ground. Unfortunately, the ring took him rather too literally. Instead of starting a gentle descent it simply switched off, causing Steve to plummet downwards like a rock.

"Aaaaaaaaaaaaaaarrrrrrrrrrrrrrrrrgggggggggggggggggg hhhhhhhhhhhh!" screamed Steve, as the ground loomed ever closer.

"Squawk squawk squawk squawk squawk," chortled the seagulls (which roughly translates as: "Well done, lads. Now, let's go and steal some chips.")

Steve plummeted downwards, the rush of wind pushing his cheeks back so that he looked like the Joker. But Steve didn't feel like laughing. He was meant to be the hero that saved the day, not end up as a pancake flattened on the ground.

The ring just wouldn't work, no matter how hard he pleaded. Steve guessed he was simply too scared to think straight. As the ground rushed up to meet him, he closed his eyes and crossed his fingers.

WUMPH!

Steve lay there, his eyes still tightly closed. Still dazed, he opened his eyes and tried to wiggle his fingers and toes. He was relieved to find that even though he ached all over, everything seemed to be still attached and in working order.

He looked around him, trying to assess his surroundings. To be honest, this wasn't what he'd expected heaven to look like. He'd *definitely* thought it would smell better.

As Steve lay there, looking up at the sun and the cackling birds circling overhead, a man's face came into view, peering down at him. He had a round bald head with a squashed red nose and a thin dark goatee. His nose crinkled with displeasure as he looked down at Steve, obviously not expecting to find him there.

"Ere, what are you doing you little scamp? Get off with you!"

Steve looked at the man in confusion. "Get off to where?" he asked.

"I don't care, do I," thundered the man, his whole face beginning to turn as red as his nose. "Just get out of my bleedin' bin!"

He threw a black bag that landed beside Steve's feet, and then stomped off muttering to himself. Wondering what on earth was going on, Steve looked inside the bag and found it filled with plastic bottles, wrappers and cans.

Steve stumbled to his feet and looked around him. He was surrounded by bin bags and rubbish and could see several other large bins lined up behind shops and restaurants. Steve looked down at his filthy clothes and tried to ignore the horrible stench coming from him, even though it made his eyes water.

Hauling himself out of the mire and onto solid ground, he trudged off towards home on foot. After what he'd just been through he was more than happy to leave flying to the birds.

When Steve finally arrived home all he really wanted was a shower and a change of clothes, but he knew that he had to move fast. Mr Spence had already brainwashed the whole school and kidnapped poor Mr Hunter. Who knew what he might do next?

Steve had always dreamed of finding himself in an exciting adventure, but now that one had arrived he felt totally out of his depth. He was just an ordinary boy not a superhero – how was he meant to fight a supervillain?

Unfortunately, Mr Hunter was the only superhero he knew, and it wasn't as if he could find the others in the phone book. But he did still have a key for Mr Hunter's house - perhaps something in the basement might help him figure out what to do next.

***

Steve had grown increasingly frustrated as he wandered around Mr Hunter's basement, trying to make sense of the objects there. He had found plenty of things that might be useful but had no idea what any of them did and wasn't sure he wanted to risk finding out. He wouldn't be much help to Peter and the others if he turned into a badger or some other mishap befell him.

Steve froze as from upstairs he heard the front door open and the sound of footsteps walking across the hall. Hardly daring to breathe, all sorts of possibilities flashed through his mind. Had Mr Spence come to find him? Had he sent one of his classmates or perhaps called the police?

"Steven, are you here?" called Mr Hunter, the familiar voice making Steve's heart leap for joy. Mr Hunter had escaped! He didn't have to do this by himself anymore!

He was about to reply, the words on the tip of his tongue, when some instinct stopped him. Mr Hunter had been a helpless prisoner the last time he'd seen him – how had he managed to escape?

"Come out wherever you are, boy. Mr Spence wants you back in his office, there's no place to hide."

The sound of the heavy footsteps moved from side to side as Mr Hunter began to search his home.

Steve groaned in despair. The voice may have been Mr Hunter's but it wasn't the kindly superhero that he'd come to know over the last few hours. It was the grumpy old man that had made his life a misery for months.

Steve had never felt so alone. Now there really was nothing he could do. He might as well just sit there and wait to be discovered.

But as he sat there expecting the worst, a thought entered his head that gave him renewed hope. Mr Hunter had been turned back into a grumpy old man – the same grumpy old man who didn't realise he had a secret lair in his basement!

The realisation helped calm Steve's frazzled nerves. He was hopefully safe for the moment, but he knew that he couldn't stay in the basement all day. Sooner or later he would have to make his move.

Steve looked around the room one more time, hoping to find something – anything – that he could use to help him. Then his gaze fell upon a glass cabinet in the corner of the room and an idea began to form in his head. With a bit of luck he might be able to get out of this mess after all.

18

THE MASTER OF DISGUISE

Mr Hunter stomped through his house like a man possessed, throwing open doors, banging cupboards and muttering to himself. A boy was hiding in his house! A smelly, dirty little boy! He'd soon find the little menace and return him to Mr Spence.

Mr Hunter couldn't remember precisely why finding the boy was so important, and felt a little tickle in his brain when he tried to recall. Still, it didn't really matter. If returning the boy to school meant that he could once again enjoy the peace and quiet of his own home, that's exactly what he'd do.

Nevertheless, there was something about Mr Spence that he couldn't quite put his finger on. Something familiar, almost as if they had met before...

He shook his head, angry at himself for getting distracted. "Where are you?" he roared. "Stop hiding, boy, and come out and face me."

"Okay," replied a small voice behind him.

"AHA!"

Mr Hunter spun round, ready to capture his prey, but was confronted by an altogether surprising sight. The boy before him was not dressed in the school uniform of Blackwood Academy but in some sort of garish fancy-dress outfit. A green t-shirt was matched with bright blue trousers and a long red cape. On the breast of the t-shirt was a yellow logo that featured an oval with the letters 'RL' inside. He looked ridiculous, like something from an infantile cartoon. Yet at the same time, something about the outfit seemed almost familiar.

The itching in Mr Hunter's head grew worse and he closed his eyes, trying to calm himself.

"What on earth are you wearing, you stupid boy?

You and I are heading back to school right now!"

The boy looked at him defiantly, his small fists tightly clenched. "I am Reason Lad," he announced, "and you are The Defender!"

Mr Hunter tried to tell the boy to stop being silly, but his mouth was suddenly dry and his head was beginning to ache as if there was a swarm of angry bees within. He closed his eyes and put his hand on the wall to steady himself.

"You're coming with me," he grunted.

What was happening to him? What was the horrid boy doing?

He opened his eyes to find the boy looking up at him. Although his blue eyes were barely visible behind the domino mask, the look of steely determination in them was clear. "No," the boy announced. "You're coming with me and we're going to save the day, because that's what heroes do."

Heroes... heroes... heroes...

The word replayed over and over in Mr Hunter's head, blocking out every other thought. He felt himself spiralling downwards and tried to summon the energy to fight one more time.

"You little menace! I'm going to take you to Mr Spence and then I'll never have to see you again."

The boy didn't flinch at the threat and looked at Mr Hunter with an expression of gentleness that only infuriated him even more.

"No, you're not. You don't hurt people. You save them. You defend them. That's what you do, you just have to remember."

The pain in Mr Hunter's head grew worse, with the pounding growing so intense that he feared his skull might explode like a cracked egg. Vivid colours danced before his eyes and beads of sweat began to run down his face.

"Mr Hunter, remember who you are I know you can do it!"

"STOP IT, just stop talking!" he shouted.

"Remember Blackwood Academy! Remember the children! Remember powers and costumes and keeping people safe! Remember that you're a hero!"

Mr Hunter roared in pain and staggered forward, clamping his hand on the boy's shoulder. "That's enough!" he gasped through gritted teeth.

The boy smiled up at him and unclenched his fist. Nestled within it was a black domino mask, aged and weathered but somehow familiar.

"Where did you get that?" Mr Hunter breathed.

"I believe in you," replied the boy. "And Mr Hunter, right now we need a hero to help us. We need someone to defend us."

Inside Mr Hunter's mind raged a battle as fierce as any supervillain fight. The Defender grappled with the grumpy old man, both of them striving for victory.

"You're not real, you're just something Billy created!"

"You're the fake! A grown man playing at dress up!"

With a terrible groan, Mr Hunter collapsed to the floor and lay still.

"MR HUNTER!" shouted Steve, tearing off his mask and running to his side. "Are you okay? Please be okay."

For a second all was still, and Steve began to fear the worst. Then Mr Hunter opened his eyes and slowly clambered to his feet. He fixed Steve with a piercing gaze and strode towards him, his arms outstretched.

It didn't work, Steve thought in despair. *He still wants to capture me.*

Mr Hunter came forward and put his hands on Steve's shoulders, grasping them tightly. Steve closed his eyes, awaiting his fate, as Mr Hunter...

Lifted him into the air and spun him round.

"WAHOOOOOOOOOOOOOOO! You did it my boy, you did it! You brought me back to normal!"

"I did?" exclaimed Steve in surprise, hardly believing what he was hearing. But then he saw Mr Hunter before him, once again full of smiles and good cheer, and realised that The Defender was back.

"I did!" Steve cheered, jigging from side to side with delight. He and Mr Hunter joined hands and skipped round in a circle, both of them giggling like madmen.

Mr Hunter was breathing heavily when they came to a stop, and patted his brow with a handkerchief that he produced from his trouser pocket. "Sorry, my boy, I'm afraid I'm not as young as I once was."

"Not to worry, Mr Hunter," Steve reassured him.

"Now you're back to normal I know that we can stop Mr Spence. I bet you've come up with a great plan."

Steve looked at Mr Hunter expectantly.

Mr Hunter looked at his shoes.

There was an awkward silence.

Steve coughed, feeling rather embarrassed. "Mr Hunter, you *do* have a plan, don't you?"

Mr Hunter mumbled something under his breath.

"I'm sorry, I didn't catch that," replied Steve.

"I said 'not really'," sighed Mr Hunter. "Billy was usually the one that came up with the clever plans, I was always better at hitting things."

Steve tried, rather unsuccessfully, to disguise his disappointment. "Well, that's okay, I'm sure we can think of something," he declared.

Mr Hunter gave him a weak smile of gratitude but it was clear that he didn't believe him. Steve wasn't sure that he believed himself either. What on earth were they going to do?

RAT A TAT TAT

The forceful knock on Mr Hunter's front door snapped Steve back to reality. For a second, he worried that Mr Spence had sent someone else to find him, before laughing at himself for being paranoid. He'd be very surprised if brainwashed zombies were polite enough to knock before entering.

Steve pulled open the door to reveal his Mum standing there, rooting around in her bag.

"Morning, Mr Hunter. Two seconds and we'll be off, I just have another form for you to fill in first."

She looked up and did a double-take when she saw Steve, her eyes growing as wide as saucers.

"Steve?" she spluttered in astonishment. "Why on earth aren't you in school? And why are you wearing that ridiculous costume?" She waved a reproachful finger at him. "You better have a good explanation for this, young man!"

"He has the best explanation there is, Mrs Grant. He's helping me save the world!"

Steve's Mum looked up at Mr Hunter, who had come to join Steve at the door, and her mouth opened and closed like a goldfish when she saw that he was wearing The Defender's domino mask.

"How about it, Mum," asked Steve. "Want to help

us save the world?"

By this point, Mrs Grant was 99% positive that she was dreaming. After all, what other explanation could there be for Steve skipping school, being at Mr Hunter's house, and for Mr Hunter being a superhero?

Yes, she was definitely dreaming, that was it.

"Sure," she said weakly, hoping that she would soon wake up in her nice, cosy bed. "Why not."

"Excellent!" boomed Mr Hunter. "Now, let's save the day!"

19

THE DOMINO CLUB

Mrs Grant, Steve and Mr Hunter all trooped on to the small yellow minibus, causing the passengers already on board - Bert, Sandra, Reg and Tony – to look up in surprise. Not only was there an oddly dressed boy, but Arthur (as they called Mr Hunter) seemed to be acting very strangely.

"Ah, my comrades in arms," he announced as he bounded down the aisle towards them. "Good morning to you all!"

Reg leaned over to Tony. "What's the matter with Arthur?" he whispered. "He actually seems happy for once."

"Dunno," Tony replied. "He maybe heard that the Age Concern has a new set of dominoes."

Mrs Grant slid into the driver's seat and closed the bus doors, before pulling on her seatbelt and staring blankly into the distance. Steve looked at her with some concern - this wasn't like her at all.

"Are you sure you're okay?" he asked. "I know this must seem pretty strange."

His Mum laughed. "Oh, I've had dreams that were a lot crazier than this one! Although I've never dreamt about Steve as a superhero before – I must remember and tell him when I wake up."

"Mum, this isn't –".

At the last second, Steve thought better of telling his Mum the truth. If she thought this was all a dream then it might be easier for her to accept all the crazy things that were going on.

He looked towards the rear of the bus, where Mr Hunter was talking to his friends. From the confused expressions on their faces and the way they exchanged worried glances, it was clear that they thought he'd gone totally loopy.

"And that's when Steve reversed the brainwashing," chuckled Mr Hunter, slapping his knee. "For the second time!"

He stopped, awaiting some kind of reaction from his audience. Instead there was only polite silence.

"That's nice, Arthur," smiled Sandra. "You have had a busy day."

"Sounds like he's forgotten to take his pills today," muttered Reg, causing Bert to stifle a snort of laughter.

"Mr Hunter," Steve called over. "Can you come here for a minute?"

Mr Hunter hurried over to join him and they sat down together. Steve leaned closer, keeping his voice low.

"We *really* need to come up with a plan. We'll be at the school soon and we need to work out what we're doing when we get there."

"My boy!" exclaimed Mr Hunter in surprise. "You're not worried, are you?"

"OF COURSE I'M WORRIED!" spluttered Steve,

turning a funny shade of pink. "Do I really have to explain why? **One** - My headteacher is a supervillain! **Two** – My friends are all brainwashed! **Three** – Our 'team' consists of four pensioners and my Mum, who thinks she's tucked up in bed dreaming! And **Four** – You don't seem the slightest bit worried!"

"Oh, I've been in worse scrapes than this before," Mr Hunter modestly replied.

"You have?" replied Steve sceptically. "Really? Name one."

"Of course," smiled Mr Hunter. "There was the time when... um, the time where... when I..."

He rubbed his chin and pursed his lips. "Hmmm. Okay, now that I think about it, this does seem to be quite a pickle."

"SEE!" shouted Steve. "That's what I've been trying to tell you!"

"Ah, but you see, young man, I'm not worried," Mr Hunter reassured him. "Good always triumphs over evil. And besides, we have the finest back-up that anyone could hope for."

He gestured towards the back of the bus where his

friends from the Age Concern were sitting. Bert was engrossed in his newspaper, Reg was slurping tea from an ancient Thermos, Sandra was knitting and Tony had fallen asleep, whistling noises sounding through the gaps in his ancient teeth.

"These guys?" said Steve, unconvinced. "Really? What are we going to do? Knit Mr Spence a nice scarf?"

"Not at all," chuckled Mr Hunter. "Oh, perhaps they don't look like much to a young fellow such as yourself, but I can't think of anyone better to help us."

Steve scrutinised them carefully, wondering what he was missing. They looked just like ordinary old people. Between them they had glasses and hearing aids, and what little hair they had left was now as white as snow.

Tony grunted in his sleep and rolled to the side, narrowly avoiding getting one of Sandra's knitting needles lodged up his nostril. Steve thought to himself that it would be a miracle if the oldies managed to stay awake, never mind defeat a supervillain.

"Okay, I give up," he exclaimed. "What's the big secret? Are they really superspies? Is Bert a ninja? Does Sandra knit grenade covers?"

Mr Hunter smiled from ear to ear, pleased that Steve had yet to guess his secret. He tapped the end of his nose and gave him a big wink.

"The answer, my dear boy, is that these men and women honour one thing above all else – fair play."

"Gee, that's great," muttered Steve sarcastically. "That'll really help us with Mr Spence."

"Just watch this," Mr Hunter reassured him. He cleared his throat loudly, waking Tony with a start and making Reg slosh tea all over his tie.

"I've got exciting news for you all. We're going on an important mission."

"Ooh, are we going to the Bingo?" squealed Sandra, clapping her hands with delight.

"No, we're going to a school."

"A school?" snorted Bert. "I don't need to go to any school, I've been to the University of life."

"It's important!" proclaimed Mr Hunter, gesturing towards Steve. "This boy needs our help. His headteacher," – he paused dramatically – "is a cheat!"

"A cheat?" whispered Steve. "What, was the supervillain part not important enough to mention?"

"I know what I'm doing," Mr Hunter urged. "Just watch this."

Steve looked again at the four oldies and immediately noticed something different. They didn't look sleepy anymore, or bored. They just looked *very* annoyed.

"A cheat!" exclaimed Reg. "And him a headteacher, no less! What an example to set."

"For shame!" shouted Bert. "The man's a blaggard and a bounder."

"He's worse than that," Sandra jeered. "He's a cheat!"

"A cheat!" roared Tony. "Let's get him!"

The four pensioners jumped out of their seats and charged to the front of the bus where they huddled round the doors, poised to leap out as soon as they opened.

Steve watched in utter amazement. "What on earth just happened?" he asked.

"Something I discovered a long time ago during a game of dominoes," confided Mr Hunter. "They really, really hate cheats and bad behaviour." He absentmindedly rubbed his arm. "I just wish I'd found that out a little earlier."

Any further explanation was curtailed as the bus shook violently, forcing Steve to grab onto a seat for support. Looking out the window he saw the surrounding streets whiz by faster and faster.

Trying to keep his footing, he slid and stumbled his way to the front of the bus.

"MUM, WHAT ARE YOU DOING?" he shouted as the bus mounted the pavement, knocking over a bin and narrowly missing a small dog that was tied up outside the chemist.

"This is a dream," his Mum happily replied, "so I can drive as fast as I want and nothing bad will happen. I wonder if I can do a wheelie?"

"NO! DON'-"

Before Steve could get the words out his Mum nudged the bus up onto the kerb and jerked the wheel. The bus lurched to the side, creaking and groaning, and Steve felt his stomach flip as the bus lifted into the air. It hung there for a few seconds before it crashed to the ground with a jolt that made his teeth judder.

Bert's false teeth went one better. They shot out of his mouth and slid along the floor, finally vanishing under a seat in the back of the bus.

"DON'T DO THAT AGAIN!" Steve shouted at his Mum. "Are you trying to get us all killed?"

"Don't be silly," laughed his Mum. "You can't die in a dream." A big grin spread over her face and she gripped the steering wheel tighter. "Oooh, there are traffic lights coming up – I've always wanted to drive through a red light. This is amazing!"

"IT'S NOT AMAZING!" shouted Steve. "It's anything but amazing and you need to stop this!"

"Here we goooooooooooo!" cheered his Mum as she steered the bus towards the traffic lights. Steve looked out of the windscreen just in time to see a very familiar looking old lady jump out of the way as the bus careered through the red light, her freshly bought replacement apples spilling all over the ground.

***

Parked nearby, PC Jones was sitting in his police car about to tuck into a large portion of fish and chips. He licked his lips as he opened the box and examined its contents. The tasty aroma filled the car, making his large round stomach gurgle with impatience.

The first chip hadn't even reached his mouth when a yellow bus raced past at high speed, honking its horn and making him jump with surprise. His fish and chips flew into the air and spilled everywhere, coating the inside of the police car in chips, batter, vinegar and sauce.

PC Jones looked down at the remnants of his tasty lunch, with the food now covered in hair and dirt, and tried very hard not to cry. Looking out of his sauce-splattered windscreen he saw the bus vanishing into the distance and could hear the driver whooping with excitement.

"Right, troublemaker," he exclaimed, pulling on his seatbelt and starting the engine. "Now you're going to see what happens when you destroy a policeman's lunch!"

He switched on the siren and swerved into the road, narrowly missing an old lady who was still trying to collect the shopping strewn all around her.

***

Steve groaned in exasperation. His Mum was acting almost as dangerously as Mr Spence! But how could he persuade her that she wasn't dreaming? Then a brilliant idea popped into his head – perhaps he didn't have to.

"MUM," Steve shouted over the roar of the engine.

"Yes, sweetie," replied his Mum as she weaved in and out of traffic, drivers shouting and beeping their horns as they swerved to avoid her.

"Even though this is a dream, you're still my Mum, aren't you?"

"Of course I am," she smiled reassuringly.

"Then shouldn't you be setting me a good example?" Steve innocently enquired. "After all, do you *really* want to teach me that we shouldn't obey the law?"

"Oh, I suppose not," sighed his Mum, sulking. "Can I at least do one more wheelie?"

"I think you should just drive to school, Mum. Nice and slowly, please."

Mrs Grant gave an exaggerated sigh and steered the bus back into the correct lane, slowing down to the speed limit. A couple of minutes later they pulled into the school carpark and she switched off the ignition.

As the chug of the engine quietened and then faded away, six heads turned to look at Steve, waiting for his signal on what to do next.

Steve barely noticed. His attention was focused on the familiar building in front of him, wondering what manner of danger awaited them inside.

They were about to find out.

20

THE BATTLE FOR BLACKWOOD ACADEMY

Steve gathered everyone close to him. "Okay, we need some kind of a plan," he told them, trying to sound braver than he felt. "We have to work together."

"What's there to talk about?" roared Bert. "The man's a cheat and we'll show him what happens to cheaters!" His friends enthusiastically shouted their agreement and Tony gave him a hearty slap on the back, sending his false teeth shooting across the bus once more.

Steve sighed. "I appreciate the enthusiasm, but he's really dangerous – he can control your mind. We have to work out a way of stopping him."

"How does he control minds, dearie?" asked Sandra.

"It's something to do with his voice," Steve told her, aware that it sounded rather silly when he said it out loud. "He tells you to do things and you can't stop yourself doing it."

"Sorry, dearie, what was that?" Sandra interrupted, fiddling with her ear. "I didn't quite catch that, I think the batteries in my hearing aid are starting to go."

"You couldn't really hear me..." muttered Steve as cogs within his mind started whirring and chugging.

An idea began to form...

"SHE COULDN'T REALLY HEAR ME!" he shouted in delight, causing everyone to stare at him in astonishment.

"Steady on, old boy," admonished Reg. "It's not her fault."

"I know that!" gushed Steve. "It's a good thing. No, it's a great thing!"

He bounced over to Mr Hunter and grabbed him by the braces, pulling him close. "Mr Hunter, don't you get it? If they can't hear Mr Spence then he can't control them!"

"Absolutely," agreed Mr Hunter. "That is a brilliant plan. 100% gold."

"I know! Can you explain it to your friends? I'm not sure they'll pay much attention to a ten-year-old."

Mr Hunter awkwardly cleared his throat, looking embarrassed. "It's not that I don't want to, and obviously I *completely understand* your plan. But since you came up with it then I think you should have the honour of telling it."

Steve wasn't entirely convinced that Mr Hunter understood, but there was no time to argue. Instead, he gestured the small group to come closer.

"Mr Spence uses his voice to control people, so what we have to do is make sure that we can't hear him. Bert, Reg, Sandra and Tony – you all have hearing aids, don't you?"

Tony self-consciously touched his ear. "I don't really need it, I'm sure I could manage without it if I wanted."

"No, no, no," Steve reassured him. "It's a good

thing, really. If you all turn your hearing aids off then Mr Spence will find it a lot harder to control you."

"What about those of us who don't have hearing aids?" asked Mr Hunter.

"We'll have to be sneaky," replied Steve. "While the oldies cause a distraction, we'll sneak into the school and set off the fire alarm. When that goes off it'll be so loud that there's no way Mr Spence can control us."

"And then we can catch him unawares!" exclaimed Mr Hunter. "Brilliant, my boy."

As Mr Hunter explained the details of the plan to his friends, Steve sought out his Mum. She was standing on the edge of the group and looking rather confused.

"Are you okay, Mum?" he asked gently.

"I'm not sure," she replied. "But now I think – I know – that this isn't a dream, is it?"

Steve took her hand and squeezed it affectionately. "Sorry, Mum. I know I shouldn't have lied to you but this isn't the easiest thing to explain."

His Mum chuckled to herself as she watched the old folk, now with their hearing aids turned off, shouting to each other at ever increasing volumes.

"It's certainly not and it's a lot to take in. But I can see that you're trying to help people and I can't tell you how proud that makes me."

"Aw, Mum, don't get soppy!" complained Steve, pulling away before she could complete her attempted cuddle.

"Right!" he shouted, desperate to change the subject. "Everyone knows what they've got to do, so let's go. We've got a school to save!"

"We've got a fool to shave?" asked Reg, giving him a most peculiar look.

"No, I said... oh, forget it, it doesn't matter."

"Look on the bright side," Mr Hunter told Steve as he ushered Reg and his companions off the bus and into the playground. "If they can't hear you then they shouldn't hear Mr Spence either."

The bus doors closed behind them with a hiss and Steve looked around him. Nothing was moving in front of the school and no one was visible through the classroom windows. Everything seemed quiet. Too quiet.

"Follow me," he whispered. "And stay close!"

With Steve's Mum bringing up the rear and doing her best to usher the pensioners forward, the group carefully inched towards the school building.

When they had almost reached the main entrance, Steve stopped and turned to face his ragtag band. "Okay, here we go. Are you all ready?"

"Are we all teddies?" repeated Reg. "What a daft question."

"No – ARE YOU READY!" bellowed Steve, causing his Mum and Mr Hunter to wince and cover their ears.

"Of course we're ready," replied Reg. "Why didn't you just say so?"

Before Steve could reply the doors to the school burst open and wave after wave of pupils poured out, heading straight towards the small group.

"Get the intruders," they repeated in dry monotone voices. "Mr Spence wants us to get the intruders." Steve could see Peter at the front of the queue, along with Jill and so many other familiar faces. But there wasn't a flicker of recognition in their eyes as they marched towards him.

"Now?" asked Mr Hunter, as the crowd drew ever closer.

"Wait for it," Steve told him, his eyes fixed on the advancing crowd.

"Now?" shouted Mr Hunter as the crowd marched onwards, their outstretched arms ready to grab their prey.

"NOW!" shouted Steve.

Mr Hunter wrapped his arms around him and they lifted into the air, rising above the heads of the grasping crowd.

"I know I shouldn't be having fun at a time like this," smiled Mr Hunter, "but by golly it's good to fly again."

"You're welcome to it," replied Steve, gesturing at the ring that was back on Mr Hunter's finger after so many years. "I think I make a better passenger than a pilot."

He looked down at the figures below as they grew ever smaller, receding into the distance. Steve hated the thought of leaving his Mum and the others behind, but he knew that this plan had the best chance of succeeding. He just hoped his hunch was correct that his classmates wanted to capture them rather than hurt them.

"Okay, head that way and land just over there."

Following Steve's directions, Mr Hunter flew them over the school and brought them down on the far side of the building, next to an emergency exit.

There was just one problem.

"There's no handle," groaned Mr Hunter in exasperation. "It must only open from the inside! What are we going to do now?"

"Don't worry," Steve reassured him. "We were never trying to go through the emergency exit – I think it's alarmed."

Smiling, he pointed toward an open window further to the side. "It's my classroom," he explained. "Mrs Baxter always insists on having the window open no matter what time of year it is."

He sidled up to the window and peeked through, breathing a sigh of relief when he saw that the classroom was empty. Hoisting himself up, he clambered through and then opened the window as wide as it would go.

Mr Hunter's entrance wasn't quite as graceful. He got stuck when he was halfway through the window and Steve had to grab his arms and pull with all his might. Eventually, after much pulling, pushing and exertion on both their parts, Mr Hunter tumbled through and landed in a heap on the floor.

"Where now?" he panted, still trying to get his breath back. "You'll remember the school layout better than I do."

"There should be a fire-alarm in the next corridor," Steve informed him. "The only problem is that it's next to Mr Spence's office."

"Then we'll have to be extra quiet. We can't fail now, there are too many people counting on us."

The school was still deathly quiet. The only sounds that Steve could make out were the ticking of the clock on the wall and muted shouts coming from the front car park. It seemed that everyone had gone to see what the commotion was.

Either that or they were lying in wait, ready to jump out and grab them.

Trying to ignore the butterflies in his stomach, Steve crept forward and opened the classroom door. Peeking out and seeing no signs of movement, he slipped into the corridor with Mr Hunter following close behind.

He could see the fire alarm ahead of him, set in a small glass case just before Mr Spence's office. The office door was open but there were no signs of movement from within. Steve hoped that it stayed that way.

Steve reached the fire alarm and readied himself to break the glass. Everything came down to this. The noise of the alarm would hopefully drown out Mr Spence and also alert the fire brigade and police, providing the reinforcements they so desperately needed. He drew back his fist.

And froze when he heard a cough behind him.

Mr Spence was leaning in the doorway to his office, a cold smile on his face.

"Steven Grant – how nice to see you again!" he declared. "And I see that you've dressed for the occasion."

"We're here to stop you, Billy," proclaimed Mr Hunter. "This can't go on – you need to stop and think about what you're doing."

"Oh, I've thought about it," answered Mr Spence. "And I've decided that I really can't have you two interfering any more. After all, who knows who could get hurt in the process?"

As Steve heard Mr Hunter gasp in surprise he made a desperate lunge for the fire alarm.

But a fist came out of nowhere and grabbed his arm in an iron grip, holding him back. Steve's heart sank when he saw that it belonged to Mr Hunter.

"Mr Hunter," he pleaded. "We're so close, you have to fight this!"

"I'm sorry, my boy," Mr Hunter choked. "I'm so sorry but I don't have a choice."

Steve glared at Mr Spence, who held his hands up in placation. "Oh, I'm not controlling his mind," he assured him. "Mr Hunter's just reconnected with an old friend, that's all."

Steve's mind filled with all sorts of terrible scenarios. Who had Mr Spence captured? His Mum?

One of the oldies? He hoped they were okay – he'd never forgive himself if his plan had led to them getting hurt.

But when someone stepped out of the shadows to join Mr Spence, it was the last person that Steve would have expected to see.

Standing beside Mr Spence, her emotionless face staring blankly ahead, was dinner lady Mary.

21

OLD FRIENDS AND NEW FOES

"LET HER GO THIS INSTANT!"

Steve had heard Mr Hunter shout many times before but he had never seen him quite this angry. His hands were tightly clenched into fists and a fire blazed in his eyes, causing even Mr Spence to take an involuntary step back before regaining his composure.

"Oh, I don't think I'll be doing that," said Mr Spence. "As long as I have Mary then I can be sure that you won't do anything stupid."

He waved a hand in front of her eyes. There was no reaction as she remained staring straight ahead, unblinking.

"Anyway, I'm doing Mary a favour. It's good for her to get out from the kitchen sometimes, don't you agree?"

"I was wrong about you," seethed Mr Hunter. "I thought that the Billy I knew was still in there somewhere, but now I see that you really have changed."

He shook his head sorrowfully. "Threatening an innocent woman... I thought you were better than that."

A look of deep hurt on Mr Spence's face was gone as soon as it appeared, masked by a flash of anger. With visible effort he regained control of his emotions and sarcastically applauded Mr Hunter.

"Oh, well done - trying to make me lose control and do something rash. The problem is, I know all of your tricks! There's nothing you can do that I'm not prepared for."

With a guttural roar, Mr Hunter leaped towards Mr Spence who simply sidestepped and grabbed him by his jersey, using the old man's momentum to slam him into the desk.

Mr Spence held him as he thrashed and struggled, unable to gain the leverage to get up. Roughly pulling the flight ring from Mr Hunter's finger, he held it up to the light and examined it with interest.

"I haven't seen this for a long time – it certainly brings back some memories. It's a shame for you that you're so old and weak now. Without this ring you're just a helpless old man."

He gestured towards the corner of the room, his attention still focused on the ring. "Now, do as you're told - go stand over there and don't move."

"I won't!" shouted Mr Hunter. "I'll stop you!" But despite his protests and attempts at resistance, his feet doggedly walked him towards the corner of the room.

Mr Spence pulled open a desk drawer and dropped the ring inside before turning his attention towards Steve. "Now, what should I do with you?" he mused.

"What's going on?" Steve asked, frantically playing for time. "Why is dinner lady Mary here? How does she know Mr Hunter?"

"Oh, you don't know!" exclaimed Mr Spence in surprise, clapping his hands together. "Oh, this is too delicious. I had thought that you two were bosom buddies but it looks like your friend still has a few secrets from you."

"What does he mean, Mr Hunter?" asked Steve. "Who is dinner lady Mary to you?"

Mr Hunter gave Steve an apologetic smile and then gazed over at Mary, his expression softening. "Only the love of my life," he whispered.

***

If you're an observant reader who had managed to put all the clues together – congratulations! Pat yourself on the back and have a cookie (But don't try and do both things at the same time or you may drop crumbs down your neck.)

If, however, you're staring at the page in utter confusion and your head is beginning to hurt, let's travel back around 40 years or so to a very different Blackwood Academy. There were no Smart Boards or ICT lessons, no mobile phones or Pokemon. But there were some familiar faces – our star-crossed lovebirds, Mr Hunter and dinner lady Mary.

It was just a typical Monday at the school when Mr Hunter went to the canteen for his lunch. Queueing for his food and examining the options before him, he automatically stuck his plate out to get filled up – then his eyes widened as he beheld the most beautiful vision of loveliness he had ever laid eyes on.

Newly arrived at the school, standing there with her dark brown hair tied back and a shy smile on her face, Mary was also taken with the man standing before her. He was tall and well-built but had a kind face, and when he managed to blurt out a 'Hello' she felt her heart skip a beat.

And that's how it started. The two saw each other in the canteen every day, separated by a glass counter, and while they were both terribly shy, each day they became a little more comfortable with each other. Shy smiles turned into friendly hellos and before long they were having the most wonderful conversations, much to the frustration of the people stuck behind Mr Hunter in the queue.

Something that children often don't realise about adults is that they can still be shy and suffer from self-doubt. And although Mr Hunter and Mary both loved spending time together, each still worried that perhaps the other didn't feel the same way.

So with neither of them brave enough to voice their feelings, they both found other ways to show their devotion. Each day, Mary would serve Mr Hunter huge portions of food, until it was almost spilling off his plate. For his part, Mr Hunter would praise the cooking, declaring it to be the best that he had ever tasted.

And that's how it might have continued indefinitely if something hadn't happened that changed everything. Mr Hunter gained superpowers and assumed the identity of The Defender.

With each person that he saved, with each disaster that he and Billy averted, Mr Hunter's confidence grew. *Soon*, he told himself. *Soon I'll tell Mary just what she means to me.*

When he next saw her at lunch they exchanged the usual pleasantries, but Mary was taken aback when Mr Hunter returned his empty plate at the end of his meal. "I'll see you tonight," he smiled. "I'll pick you up here at 17.30."

Mary spent the rest of the day in a dream. Lost in her happy thoughts she piled food onto plates, barely paying attention to what had been requested. And when lunch time was over she cleared tables and washed dishes with a spring in her step, whistling a merry tune. She couldn't wait until 17:30 – after all this time the night was finally here!

And at 18:00 a dejected Mary began her long walk home, feeling like her heart had been broken in two. Mr Hunter – her beloved Arthur – had never shown and hadn't even had the decency to get in touch.

What Mary didn't know was that at the same time Mr Hunter was meant to meet her, his memory – his very self – was being altered by Billy Spence. By the time that Billy left Mr Hunter's house his old mentor had no recollection of having worked in the school, or meeting the pretty dinner lady that he had come to love.

And after Billy Spence stood up at assembly the

next day and spoke to the entire school, no-one there could remember Arthur Hunter either.

***

"That's horrible," breathed Steve. "How could you do that to them?"

Steve felt suddenly ashamed. He'd never really thought of Mary as a person, had never seen her as anything other than a grumpy old lady who served up terrible food.

"Horrible?" scoffed Mr Spence. "I'll tell you what's been horrible – having to put up with her cooking for all of these years. I think deep down some part of her must have remembered Mr Hunter, because she wouldn't stop making his favourite food."

"Mince!" exclaimed Steve, another piece of the puzzle coming together. Mince had been a permanent feature on the menu because it had been Mary recalling her lost love.

It still didn't make it taste any better though.

"Don't worry, boy," chided Mr Spence. "Soon you'll be back eating mince and you won't recall any of this ever happening."

Steve desperately looked around the room, hunting for anything that could help him. Mary was still standing in a trance, Mr Hunter was trapped in the corner of the room, and there was no bell to save him this time. There was nowhere to run - or nowhere to fly, come to think of it.

With no other option, Steve decided to do something else entirely: stand his ground and give Mr Spence a piece of his mind. Because if he was going to forget everything there were some things that he needed to say first. And besides, how often would he get the chance to tell an adult – especially a headteacher – exactly what he thought of them?

"Do you know what you are?" he asked Mr Spence, standing up straight and attempting to project a confidence that he didn't feel.

"Oh, do tell," replied Mr Spence. "I'd love to hear words of wisdom from a ten-year-old."

"You're a coward," Steve said. "A coward and a bully."

Silence filled the room. Mr Spence looked agog at Steve, his mouth hanging open in disbelief.

"Oh, I am, am I?" he replied through gritted teeth. "Any more words of wisdom that you'd like to share? I'll just warn you now that you're going to be in detention for the rest of your school life and you won't even remember why."

"You're scared that people won't like you for who you are, that's why you try and control them. But that's stupid – just be yourself! Mr Hunter thought you were his friend and I thought you were a decent headteacher – did you really need to control anybody?"

Mr Spence's eyebrows had shot up so far that they were in danger of escaping his face. He was breathing heavily, like a bull about to charge, and Steve half expected steam to come out of his ears. Swallowing hard, he continued.

"I know that some people think I'm a daydreamer or that I'm not very bright, but I'm happy with who I am. And I think that if I tried to be something I'm not – well, I think I'd just be miserable."

Steve spoke quickly, determined to get the words out. "Just answer me one thing, Mr Spence, then you can do what you want to me. You have this power and you've been able to use it to get things you want, but has it made you happy?"

Steve gestured towards Mr Hunter. "Or was your happiest time with him? When you were doing good and helping people."

Mr Spence screwed his eyes shut and shook his head from side-to-side.

"NO!" he shouted. "You're trying to trick me, trying to talk your way out of this. You don't care about me! No-one cares! Now I'm going to take care of you once and for all."

"I'm sorry, Mr Hunter," whispered Steve. "I really thought we could do this."

"Don't worry my boy," Mr Hunter consoled him, smiling kindly. "I couldn't have asked for any more from you, you're a good lad."

"What touching last words," mocked Mr Spence. "A shame that you won't remember them!"

Steve closed his eyes as Mr Spence began to speak, awaiting the inevitable.

22

THE LAST STAND

BANG!

The office door burst open and both Steve and Mr Spence jerked round in surprise.

Framed in the doorway were Steve's Mum and the oldies.

They looked a little worse for wear - Reg's glasses were bent and Sandra's perfectly permed hair was now looking rather bedraggled. But they were here! They were okay!

Steve felt like crying with happiness as he exchanged smiles with his Mum. He didn't think he'd ever been so relieved to see her.

"What is this?" thundered Mr Spence. "How did you manage to get past all the pupils under my control?"

"You're not the only one who knows how children's minds work," grinned Mrs Grant. "Between us we had enough sweets to create the perfect distraction."

Steve ran over and hugged his Mum tight, pressing his face against her. "I'm so glad you're here," he whispered. "I was scared that something might have happened to you."

"Nothing could ever stop me helping you," his Mum reassured him. "That's what Mums do."

"I hate to break up this touching scene," interrupted Mr Spence, "but you've still lost. One word from me and you'll forget all about this. All I have to say is-"

"CHEAT!"

Tony shuffled towards Mr Spence, followed by the rest of his friends. Bert was angrily waving his walking stick in the air, while Sandra spun her handbag around her head at increasing speed.

"Oh, please, is this the best you can do?" yawned

Mr Spence, looking entirely unconcerned. "Stop there," he commanded.

A flicker of doubt crossed his face as the small group continued towards him, oblivious to his commands.

"I SAID STOP," he shouted, beginning to back away.

Tony, Bert and Sandra continued to advance, but Reg started hopping on one foot. "'Here," he shouted. "What's going on?"

"DO NOT MOVE!"

Tony stopped in his tracks and thrust his arms into the air before twirling, leaping and thrusting across the floor like a contestant on Strictly. "Look at me," he called in delight. "I'm in the groove! I haven't moved like this in years!"

Bert and Sandra were almost upon Mr Spence, who was now pressed against his desk, his grasping hands knocking over its contents as he fumbled for anything that could help him.

"LISTEN TO ME!" he screeched.

Sandra's nose wrinkled with distaste. "You are a disgusting young man – how dare you!" She swung her handbag high in the air and brought it down on Mr Spence's head again and again. He covered his head with his hands and curled into a ball, trying to protect himself from the blows.

"STO – **OW!**"

"DON'T HI – **EEH!**"

"GET AWA – **AHH!**"

Every one of Mr Spence's attempted commands was cut off by a well-placed blow from Sandra's handbag, which she wielded with deadly accuracy.

The small office was in chaos, filled to bursting with people. Mr Hunter was still stuck in the corner and Mary remained in her trance, but Reg was still hopping to-and-fro while Tony danced and stomped around the room like some sort of graceful hippo.

"What do we do?" Steve's Mum asked him. "We can't keep hitting him with a handbag all day."

Steve watched Sandra deliver another hearty wallop to Mr Spence's noggin. He was pretty sure that she'd be happy to keep hitting him for some time yet. Still, perhaps there was a better option...

"I have an idea," he said. "Have you got anything that you can use to cover his mouth?"

His Mum ran over to Mary and began rifling through the pockets of her apron. She triumphantly pulled out an old dishcloth and threw it over to Steve, before setting to work on untying the apron strings.

Steve gestured for Reg and Tony to come help and the two men hopped and danced their way over. Working together with Bert, they managed to push Mr Spence onto his chair while Sandra kept up a constant stream of whacks with her handbag. Steve crammed the end of the dishcloth into Mr Spence's mouth while his Mum used the apron to tie his arms behind his back, fastening the ends to the leg of the chair.

"Mph mmph mph!"

Steve surveyed his handiwork with satisfaction before signalling everyone to turn their hearing aids back on. Mr Spence was securely tied, with the gag stopping him speaking. They'd done it! They'd won!

"WHAT ON EARTH IS GOING ON HERE?" shouted a voice from the door. "UNTIE THAT MAN!"

Oh, poo, thought Steve.

23

THE BEST LAID PLANS

PC Jones was *not* in the best of moods. He was tired, grumpy, and very hungry. After the speeding bus had ruined his lunch break he'd driven all over town hunting for it. He'd zoomed along streets, swerved round roundabouts and checked every car park he could think of, but the bus was nowhere to be found.

He pulled his police car into a layby and turned off the engine. Drumming his fingers on the steering wheel, he thought about what to do next, trying to ignore the loud gurgles coming from his hungry tummy.

He hadn't seen the number plate for the bus or caught the face of the driver, so finding it would likely be a needle in a haystack. Perhaps if he thought about who might use buses in the town.

PC Jones lay back and closed his eyes, thinking hard - something that was rather unusual for him. *Who would be transported on a bus?* he wondered. His eyes snapped open when the answer hit him: old people or school pupils!

As the school day was already underway he visited the Age Concern and the Old Folks home first, but there was no sign of the bus. Disappointed, he set off back to the police station, but as he drove past Blackwood Academy he spotted the elusive bus parked out front.

The tyres on his vehicle squealed in protest as he roared into the school grounds, screeching to a halt in the middle of the playground (For some reason he couldn't quite fathom, the car park was inaccessible due to countless children on their hands and knees picking up sweets). Shaking his head at the standard of discipline within schools nowadays, he hurried inside the building.

There was no one at reception and the building seemed suspiciously quiet; the corridors and classrooms were empty with not a soul to be seen. The only noise was faint shouting from the other end of the corridor and he hurried in that direction, clutching his radio tightly.

When he reached his destination, PC Jones was taken aback by what he found. An old man was standing in the corner laughing to himself, while several other pensioners were exchanging handshakes and hearty congratulations. For some strange reason one of them was hopping up and down, while another appeared to be dancing.

Even stranger was that a small boy appeared to be dressed as a superhero in some form of garish costume. But it was what he saw next that made PC Jones drop his radio in shock. The school headteacher, Mr Spence, was gagged and tied to a chair, the others ignoring his muffled cries for help.

Ducking out of sight, PC Jones pressed himself against the wall and fretted over what to do next. It was obvious that some kind of revolt had taken place. The children had probably risen up against their teachers and taken over, likely due to the quality of school dinners. The thought made him hungry again.

Revolting children? Criminal pensioners? Teachers being held hostage? He decided that this was *definitely* too much for him to deal with alone. He would have to call for help.

He bent down to pick up his radio, only to find to his horror that it lay smashed and useless on the floor. He swallowed hard as realisation hit him. He would have to do this himself.

PC Jones wasn't a brave man. In fact, he was really rather cowardly. But he was very hungry and knew that the sooner he dealt with this the sooner he could get some food. Licking his lips, he ran into the room.

"WHAT ON EARTH IS GOING ON HERE?" he shouted. "UNTIE THAT MAN!"

***

Steve and his Mum looked at each other in shock. Getting arrested had not been part of their plan.

"Constable, this is not what it looks like," Mrs Grant

assured him, flashing her most charming smile.

PC Jones edged his way towards Mr Spence, making sure to keep the others in sight. "Really?" he exclaimed. "Because it looks to me like you and your wrinkly friends have tied up a headteacher. Let me guess - did he give your son a bad grade? You couldn't handle him getting a C on a Maths test, could you? You parents are always the same, blame the teachers rather than the- **OW!"**

He staggered back in shock as Sandra whacked him over the head with her handbag.

"What was that for?" he spluttered. "You can't assault a policeman!"

"I can if he's being a silly sausage," declared Sandra sternly. "I know your mother, Kenneth Jones, and she would be most disappointed if she heard you being so disrespectful to your elders."

"I wasn't! I was trying to rescue Mr- **OW!"**

Sandra bonked him on the bonce one more time.

"Not even going to apologise? For shame, young Kenneth!"

PC Jones felt there was something very wrong

here. He had thought he was the good guy saving the day, yet somehow he seemed to be the bad guy. He just didn't know what was happening anymore. All he knew for sure was that he was now very hungry *and* had a really sore head.

"I'm sorry," he muttered sheepishly.

"I should think so, too!" announced Sandra, giving him one final bash. "But it takes a big man to admit his mistakes so we'll call that the end of it."

"Thank you," mumbled PC Jones, by this point wishing that he'd just made sandwiches for his lunch.

"There is one thing you could do for us," said Steve. "Could you round up all the pupils and staff and get them to gather in the assembly hall?"

***

Ten minutes later, PC Jones returned. "They should all be there," he told the assembled crowd. "But they're a really strange bunch if you don't mind me saying so," – and here he looked nervously at Sandra. "They hardly said a word; almost looked right through me."

"Yes, well there's a very good reason for that," Steve informed him. And then he – along with helpful interventions from Mr Hunter and the room's other occupants – began to fill PC Jones in on the day's strange events.

By the time that Steve had finished his story the confused copper was slumped in the corner of the room with his head in his hands, fully convinced that he had lost his marbles and gone *completely* doolally. Superheroes! Special rings! Magic socks! Evil teachers! The whole thing sounded absolutely crazy.

Well, except perhaps the last part.

"I know it sounds bonkers," admitted Steve, "but it really is the truth. Now all we need you to do is make Mr Spence undo it."

With a deep sigh that came up from his boots, PC Jones hauled himself to his feet and trudged over to Mr Spence, who was still bound and gagged in the chair. He knelt down beside him and addressed him in his most authoritative voice.

"Sir, I have been informed of a whole list of allegations which do not paint you in a good light at all. Now, if you want to help yourself I suggest that you use your 'magic voice' and return everyone back to normal. Is that clear?"

Mr Spence vigorously nodded his head.

"One more thing, Sir," added PC Jones. "If you attempt any funny business then I understand that this lady next to me is highly skilled in the use of the handbag." PC Jones rubbed his tender head. "And speaking from personal experience, Sir, I strongly recommend that you don't get on her bad side."

Sandra twirled her handbag round her head and gave Mr Spence a big wink. A bead of sweat formed on his forehead as he furiously nodded his acceptance.

PC Jones carefully removed the gag from Mr Spence's mouth while Sandra and the others kept a watchful eye on him. Steve pressed the button on the intercom and waited on tenterhooks to hear what Mr Spence would say.

For a moment there was silence and Steve began to worry that he might be thinking up a plan to escape or turn the tables, Instead, what Mr Spence said was short and to the point.

"Hello everyone, this is Mr Spence speaking.

Anything I have told you to do in the past, please disregard, and anything I have made you forget, please remember now.

"And one more thing" – and here his eyes flicked towards Mr Hunter. "Please know that I'm sorry."

When he was satisfied that Mr Spence had finished talking, PC Jones stuffed the cloth back in his mouth.

"Did it work?" he asked Steve. "Are things fixed?"

Steve looked around the room. Reg had stopped hopping and had collapsed into a chair, while Tony was deep in conversation with Bert. Then he spotted Mr Hunter emerge from the corner of the room and hesitantly approach Mary. She was looking around her in a daze, obviously wondering who all these strange people were, but her eyes grew wide as saucers when she caught sight of Mr Hunter.

The two stood facing each other, just gazing into each other's eyes without a word. Then they both began laughing and wrapped each other in a tight embrace that they held for a long time.

"Yeah," smiled Steve. "I think that things are finally fixed now."

24

THE END OF THE BEGINNING

Things moved quickly after that. Mr Spence's message had turned the pupils and staff within the assembly hall back to normal. They lined the corridors to watch him be escorted away by PC Jones, trying to come to terms with the fact that their headteacher had been an evil supervillain.

The braver souls shouted at him as he passed, provoked by memories of stolen toys, pilfered pocket money or other indignities. But the vast majority just watched him shuffle past with his head bowed and felt rather sad. They had trusted him: had believed that he was looking out for them and the school.

After Mr Spence had been taken away, Steve and Mr Hunter had prised open the large filing cabinet behind his desk and found an Aladdin's cave of treasure. It seemed like everything that Mr Spence had taken over the years was inside, with the shelves crammed full of toys, money and jewellery. Steve spotted his Mum's ring and handed it to her, before retrieving a pile of his toys.

But finding this haul of treasure didn't make him feel the excitement he'd expected. Instead, he was surprised to find that he almost felt sorry for Mr Spence. He had controlled so many people and taken their belongings, but why? The crammed filing cabinet suggested that he didn't do it for money or glory but instead just because he could.

Mr Hunter walked over and put a comforting arm round Steve's shoulder. The two of them stood in silence, staring at the huge array of contraband.

"You knew him better than anyone, Mr Hunter. Why do you think he did all this?"

Mr Hunter was silent for a moment, mulling over

his reply. "I wish I knew, Steven, but I like to think that he was lonely rather than bad. Perhaps if I'd been around I might have been able to help. That's certainly what I'm going to do now."

Steve looked at him in surprise. "You're going to help him? After everything that he's done?"

"I'm going to try," replied Mr Hunter. "We were so close at one time – he was almost like a son to me. I can't believe that idealistic boy is gone entirely."

"Superheroes must only use their powers for good and to help others," smiled Steve.

Mr Hunter chuckled. "That's right. This caper has shown me that I'm far too old to be a superhero anymore, but I'll still try and help people in any way that I can."

Steve looked up at his neighbour – the old man that he'd been scared of for so long – and impulsively threw his arms around him.

The office was quieter by this point. The oldies had returned to their bus shortly after Mr Spence's broadcast, claiming that all the excitement had made them tired. His Mum had gone to drive them home, but not before making Steve promise that he would head home soon – and *not* by flying.

Dinner lady Mary came over to Mr Hunter and interlocked her fingers with his. "Steven, I want to thank you so much," she smiled. "I can't believe that I've got my Arthur back."

She leaned closer and gave him a conspiratorial wink. "I'll never forget what you've done for us. You can have extra helpings of mince anytime you want!"

"Yum," Steve replied, trying to sound enthusiastic. "That's *great*, thanks."

***

After saying his heartfelt goodbyes to Mr Hunter and Mary, Steve went looking for his friends, trying his best to ignore the curious glances and snickering that his superhero costume attracted. He eventually found Peter sitting with Jill Mckenzie in their empty classroom, and he somehow wasn't surprised to see that they were holding hands.

"Steve!" shouted Peter, jumping to his feet and dropping Jill's hand like a hot potato. "It's great to see you – we're so glad you're okay."

He gave Jill a nudge in the side. "Aren't we, Jill?"

"Yes, well done," Jill sighed, rolling her eyes. "Much as I hate to admit it, you seem to have saved the day."

She looked him up and down and the familiar smirk returned. "Although your taste in clothing appears to have gotten worse."

Peter watched nervously as Jill and Steve stared at each other, anticipating the flow of insults that would soon resume. Instead, he was gobsmacked – and incredibly relieved - to see the two of them burst into laughter.

"I really am sorry about trying to capture you, you know," confessed Peter as the three of them discussed the day's strange events. "Part of it seems like a dream, like I was watching someone else do these things." He paused as a thought occurred to him. "Hey, did I see you *flying*?"

"Is that really a surprise?" grinned Jill. "Steve's had his head in the clouds for as long as I've known him."

As Steve chatted and bantered with his old friend and the old foe he was only now getting to know, he thought how lucky he was to have them in his life, thinking once again about Mr Spence.

"Are you okay?" asked Peter gently. "You've had a really hard day."

"I'm fine," Steve reassured him. "I'm just trying to take everything in. Mr Spence might have turned everyone in the school back to normal, but who knows who else he's used his power on in the town."

"There's a simple solution to that," suggested Jill. "Strap him to the back of a truck and drive him through town with a megaphone. That'll soon fix things."

"I wonder..." mused Peter. "You mentioned that Mr Spence had used his powers to make supervillains reform. What if they get their memories back?"

"I don't think we have anything to worry about – even if they were still in the town, they'd probably be ancient by now."

"I suppose you're right," chuckled Peter. "And who ever heard of a pensioner supervillain?"

"Absolutely," Steve smiled. "It's about as likely as having a supervillain next door."

Laughing and joking, the three friends left the

classroom, the sound of their laughter following them down the school corridor.

25

THE DOMINO CLUB: REVISTED

In the sitting room of Shady Vale Retirement Home, life continued as normal. In the corner of the room a small group of residents sat around the television. Engrossed in an episode of Bargain Hunt, they enthusiastically debated whether objects were hidden treasures or an utter waste of money.

Elsewhere, people drank cups of tea and read the papers, or faced each other in super competitive games of dominoes. But some of the usual participants weren't taking part today. In the corner of the room, Reg, Bert, Tony and Sandra sat huddled around a table, keeping their voices low.

"What a day," groaned Reg. "My feet are still aching from all that hopping."

"At least you only had to hop," grumbled Tony. "Have you any idea what it's like doing a high kick at my age? I'm going to feel that in the morning, I can tell you."

Sandra struck the edge of her tea cup with a spoon, the shrill taps interrupting the men's complaints.

"Never mind that, gents. I think the important thing is what we've discovered today."

"That Mr Hunter was The Defender and Mr Spence was Reason Lad," said Reg. "Who would have thought it?"

"I know, it's hard to believe that we've been playing dominoes with a superhero for all these years," mused Tony.

Sandra took a long sip of tea, before carefully replacing her cup in its saucer. "Yes, but imagine if he had known that he was playing dominoes against his greatest enemies!"

"To be fair, we didn't know either," Reg corrected her. "I can't believe that boy would make us forget who we were. I mean, that's like something a supervillain would do!"

"I resent that implication," countered Tony. "I happen to think that you can be a supervillain and still have a strong code of ethics."

"I'm not sure," challenged Bert. "I mean, the clue is in the name. One time- "

"QUIET!"

The others stopped talking and stared at Sandra. There was a menacing glint in her eye as she looked at them, one hand resting on top of her handbag.

"What has happened is unimportant. The boy made us forget who we were all these years ago, but fate has brought us together in this retirement home. Now that we finally have our memories restored, I think we should make up for lost time."

The others stared at her in astonishment. Reg tapped his hearing aid to make sure he'd heard correctly.

"Not that I'm disagreeing, you understand," asked

Tony, "But what exactly do you mean by 'making up for lost time'?"

"Getting back to what we do best," replied Sandra with a grin. "Everyone thinks that we're long gone, the sidekick has been arrested and The Defender is a weak old man. Who is there to stop us? Surely not a silly boy in an ill-fitting costume!"

She smiled and raised her cup into the air. "A toast, gentlemen, to the return of supervillains after all this time. Today the Retirement Home, tomorrow the town, and after that – who knows?"

They clinked their cups together, toasting their evil plans for the future.

THE END... for now

ABOUT THE AUTHOR

I am able to leap tall buildings with a single bound, have the proportionate speed and strength of a spider, and strike terror into the hearts of evildoers…

Actually, that's not quite true – despite my best efforts I've yet to develop superpowers, or find a cool secret lair. But what I do love is writing about superheroes and their wild and wonderful world.

'The Supervillain next door' is my first children's book, and I hope you've enjoyed it!

For information on future projects, check out
www.garysmithbooks.com